FALLEN ANGEL

DAVID B. RILEY

Hadrosaur Productions, Mesilla Park, NM

Fallen Angel
Hadrosaur Productions
First date of publication: February 2019

Based on characters which have appeared in *The Two Devils, The Devil's Due* and *The Dust Devil* by David B. Riley; collectively reprinted in *The Devil Draws Two*.

ISBN-10: 1-885093-86-1
ISBN-13: 978-1-885093-86-8

Hadrosaur Productions
P.O. Box 2194
Mesilla Park, NM 88047-2194
www.hadrosaur.com

In an 1897 survey for *McAll's* magazine, a majority of Americans reportedly believed there was life on Mars. What if they were right?

FALLEN ANGEL

1
SISTERS

1863
Union encampment near Vicksburg, Mississippi

Otis jabbed Cletus in the shoulder blade and pointed. "That one of them new nurses?"

His brother grinned. "Wouldn't mind getting some nursing from her."

Jeremiah started making that snorkeling sound he did. No one was sure if it was laughter or something else. "Let's go get some of that."

The nurses were staying in a wooden shack behind the barn that had been converted into an infirmary. The other two nurses didn't seem to be around.

Otis opened the door and they all went right in. The nurse was sitting on a cot, with nothing on but a petticoat. Dang she was pretty. Her silken blond hair went down to her shoulders. Her figure looked like one of those foreign opera singers they'd seen up in Nashville. She turned toward them. Her eyes sparked like emeralds. "Are you boys lost?" she asked. Her voice was deep for a woman, and cool. If she had any fear of the McAllen Brothers she sure didn't act like it.

"Nope." Jeremiah did that snickering again.

"Gentlemen, why you think I'd want the likes of the three of you is beyond me. I doubt any of you have ever had a bath in your entire lives. The livestock pen smells better than you three. Why don't go back to your tent and jerk each other off. I assure you, you can't handle me."

"You gonna let her talk to us like that?" Otis asked his brother, Cletus.

"No we are not," Cletus insisted.

A minute later the sentry heard loud screams coming from the nurse's quarters. He cocked the hammer on his Springfield single shot rifle and started for the shack. The screaming stopped. He relaxed a little. Then three soldiers came running by. He followed them into the infirmary. One of them had a broken arm. The other two had broken fingers. Blood was gushing from Otis McAllen's broken nose.

"What have we here?" Doc Clampett asked.

"These three losers got beat up by a girl," the sentry announced.

After they were mended, they waddled down to the mess tent. They did not escape the watchful eye of General Ulysses S. Grant. He approached the doctor. "That nurse, she scares me sometimes."

"She scares us all," Doc Clampett agreed. "Maybe we should send her to the other side and let her look after Johnny Reb's wounded."

Grant waved his cigar in the air. "Now that's an idea."

As the sun lowered below the horizon, Grant retrieved his favorite bottle from his tent. If Kentucky ever joined the Confederacy, he might have to up and see what he could get from Bobbie Lee in the way of a position. But, for the moment, he had a good supply of Kentucky bourbon on hand.

He noticed a very attractive woman was fiddling around with some camera equipment over by the campfire. He decided to join her. "Evening."

"Evening, General," Mabel replied.

"I doubt I'll ever understand what sort of voodoo you do to get images out of that camera of yours."

"It's not voodoo," Mabel said. "It's magic." She grinned. "Seriously, it is simple science. Certain chemicals react to light and that helps me catch an image on a thin photo plate."

Damn he liked redheads. And she was about the prettiest one he'd ever laid eyes on. If only he wasn't married. "I saw some of your photographs in town this morning."

"At the portrait store?"

"Yes."

"Well, most folks are too busy worrying about things to go and buy my pictures," Mabel said. "Place will soon likely be a burned-out hell hole and I'll likely never see the pictures again."

He found himself gazing into her cobalt blue eyes. "Well, why do you do it?"

"It's got to be told."

"I suppose so. But, is it safe? You're a woman all by yourself."

She smiled for a moment. "I seem to manage." She thought for a bit. "In all frankness, in many ways, I prefer the Confederate soldiers to yours."

"Why is that?" Grant asked.

"They're very polite. They say 'thank you' if I just offer a glass of water. And call me ma'am and open doors for me. Your guys just gimmee, gimmee and then let us rip your dress and have a feel."

"Sounds like your sister got some of that tonight," Grant said.

"Oh dear. Were the soldiers all right?" Mabel asked.

"Sure. A few broken bones and a busted nose, nothing Doc Clampett can't tend to."

"Well, Kevin isn't going to take an affront to her honor. That's just not going to happen."

"Well, maybe we should put her on the front lines. If only she wasn't a woman." Grant took a sip of his bourbon. "She's causing more casualties than Johnny Reb."

"Well, General, putting her on the front line might be unfair. Really unsporting of you." Mabel started giggling as she thought about her sister beating up the rebels.

He snuffed his cigar out. "I guess I'll turn in."

"Good night, General."

"Good night, Mabel."

The charming town they'd gone through had been nearly deserted. It wasn't considered worth fighting over. Now Vicksburg, with its strategic location on the Mississippi and major rail lines … well, that was worth fighting over. And Grant's troops had the town surrounded. Confederate General Pemberton was trapped. He couldn't get his men out of the city in time and was now part of the siege. It wasn't the type of battle they wanted to fight, but the stakes were too high to leave the city to the North.

Kevin relaxed on her cot. She had volunteered to do the night shift. There weren't that many wounded—yet. Then she heard something and saw an eye peering through the wall. She ran for the door. Another one of the boys in blue. She tackled him.

"Help!" he yelled in terror.

"You need help? Picking on a defenseless woman. You pervert." She reached down inside his britches. "I oughtta rip this thing clean off of you."

The soldier on the ground started crying.

"What the hell." She looked at him for a moment. "How old are you?"

"Twelve."

"Twelve? How can you enlist if you're twelve?"

"I'm a bugler."

She let go of his member and stood up. "I don't know whether to kill you or just spank you." She started unbuttoning his britches. "Well, maybe we'll settle on your virginity."

"Oh please. I'm scared."

"Then you shouldn't sneak around trying to look in ladies rooms."

"But you're so pretty."

"You think I'm pretty?"

"Prettiest thing I ever laid eyes on," he insisted.

Bugler Willie McCoy sat himself down by one of the many campfires. Daylight was coming in fifteen minutes. He was ready for it. A few of the older soldiers had been up drinking all night. Most of the men were asleep somewhere.

Bugler Willie McCoy had no one to tell about his latest adventure. No one would likely believe him anyway. The prettiest girl he'd ever seen kissed him. It was a simple kiss, nothing remarkable. But he'd never been kissed before.

While the McAllen brothers had the casts and bandages for their memory of the pretty nurse, Willie had his memories. Right on the lips. The war was turning out okay. Ma had been wrong.

It was time. He stood up on a box. As if an extra foot made any difference, and blasted out Reveille. All but the last note, anyway. A Confederate cannonball exploded before he could play the last note. And pieces of Willie sprayed all over the men sitting next to the fire. They didn't notice because they were dead as well.

"Captain," the sentry yelled, "we got some woman here."

Captain Robert Sinclair scratched his salt and pepper beard. "Private, I can see that. What does she want?"

"She wants to come past our pickets. Claims to be a photo … grapher." The private handed him a folded piece of paper.

The captain unfolded it and put on his spectacles. He could no longer read without them. He read the letter a second time, then a third. "Miss Saunders, you're a photographer?"

"Yes," Mabel replied. "This wagon has my equipment."

"We're an artillery unit? Wouldn't you rather go to a more active area on the front line?"

"I think this will do for now, Captain."

He shrugged. "Suit yourself."

"May I have my letter of introduction back, kind sir?" She smiled at him. She was so pretty.

He handed it back to her. He looked around. All the men were gawking at Mabel, none of them were shooting any of their cannons. "Get back to work. Ain't you numbskulls ever seen a woman before?"

As the cannons roared back to life, the colonel rode up on his black stallion. "What's the problem?"

"Nothing, sir," the captain reported. "All fixed now."

"Who's that woman?" the colonel asked.

"She's a photographer."

"A woman photographer? Never seen that before." The colonel scratched his head. "How do we know she ain't a union spy?"

"Oh, she has a letter of introduction," the captain said.

"A letter of introduction? Really?" The colonel looked over at Mabel, then back at the captain. "Who wrote this so-called letter of introduction? Who thinks we should let her just wander around our battlefield? God? Did God write her a letter?"

"Uh, close," the captain said. "The letter was signed by General Ulysses S. Grant."

The colonel nearly fell off his horse. "You're telling me she shows up past our pickets with a letter from Grant and you just let her proceed?"

"Yes, sir."

The colonel looked at his uniform for a moment. "This is gray? It hasn't turned blue? What did Grant say, exactly?"

"That she's a photographer and he didn't want us to think she was a spy."

"How nice of him," the colonel said.

Curly popped another biscuit into his mouth. These were actually fresh. The pretty blond lady baked them. And the stew. There was meat in it. Plenty of meat—not some scrawny rabbit being stretched out to feed a hundred men.

"Boy they haven't been feeding you. You're practically starving."

"Well, as we've moved farther into the south, our supply lines have been harder to maintain. The rebs, they've burned a lot of their own warehouses to keep us from getting anything." Curly pointed a finger at Vicksburg. "They ain't got nothin' to eat and civilians to feed."

"I guess it's all how you look at it," Kevin said.

"Ain't that the truth." Curly took another bite of stew. "Dang this is good."

"Wild leeks. I couldn't believe my luck. There's food out there if you go and look for it."

"And meat?"

"And meat," Kevin said. "Meat's the easy part."

"What you call this?" Curly asked.

"Johnnie Reb stew."

"Why them?"

"It's just the recipe," Kevin insisted.

After supper was out of the way, she headed back toward the nurse's quarters. She caught a whiff of cigar smoke.

"Uh, Kevin, my name is Ulysses Grant."

"Oh, a pleasure to meet you," she said.

"Everyone's talking about how you helped out with the evening mess tonight."

"Just trying to be useful, General."

"Well, I didn't get any of your stew. It was all gone before I realized we had something different than jerky and hard tack."

"It wasn't that much. I found some wild growing leeks and a tuber that almost passes for carrots. The bears love them."

"How'd you learn all that?" he asked.

"Just had a good teacher, I guess. I need to turn in, General. I have a nursing shift in a few hours."

"Well, I won't keep you. Goodnight." Grant headed back toward his tent.

2
FOOD

Kevin wasn't surprised that her room was not empty. Mabel did not look happy.

"So, was taking pictures of Johnny Reb any different than the Union boys?"

"Not really," Mabel admitted.

"A shame. And you went all the way over there. I cooked dinner for the men."

"So I heard."

"What's your problem?" Kevin asked.

"You fed them their own fallen comrades."

Kevin pointed her index finger at her sister. "Not true."

"You called it Johnny Reb Stew."

"Dang tootin'. I only used Confederate bodies for meat. I didn't serve a single blue coat. So what *is* your problem?"

"You think it's right to cook people and not tell them what they're eating?"

"I sure do. They'll get upset if they learn they're cannibals. They're all out there sleeping, bellies full. I did my part. And those bodies would've gone rotten in a few more hours. Everyone wins."

"There is something wrong in your head."

"Well, I have a nursing shift."

"Whatever." Mabel went back to her wagon and curled up in a small space she'd made for herself on those rare times when she wanted to sleep.

Sleep, in this case, lasted four minutes. Then the Union artillery battery opened up on Vicksburg. A few minutes after that, the counter barrage came flying in from the Confederate positions.

And her sister was cooking human bodies and serving them to the men. Mabel had no idea what to do with her sister. And this war was not going to end anytime soon—in spite of General Grant's assurances to the American people that it

8

would. The South was tough.

She opened up the bottle of bourbon and took a really big swig. General Grant wouldn't miss one bottle. And the war would be bad enough even if she did not have Kevin to deal with. If only Kevin would go back to hell. But Mabel had no real power over her sister. They were both angels banished from heaven. It wasn't like God was going to intervene. And Nick, they hadn't seen him in over a year.

Johnnie Reb Stew. Mabel managed a little snicker. As the artillery exploded around her, she drifted off to sleep. It was the only refuge she had from this horrible war.

Then they were playing Reveille again. Young Peter Matthews, age 13, had been some colonel's valet. Then someone handed him a bugle, a bugle with lots of scorching on it, and told him to play. It wasn't bad. It was recognizable as Reveille. Some guy threw a dried biscuit at him, but missed. A raven flew off with the biscuit. Then some nurse kissed him. She was crying and she kissed him. He had no idea what that was about. "What's for breakfast, Curly?"

"Got some of that Johnny Reb Stew left from last night. Kevin came up with some bacon. Got some flapjacks."

"Flapjacks and bacon. Lay it on me," the new bugler decided. It was nice they were getting some meat now and then. As the army moved deeper into Mississippi the supply problems kept getting worse. Perishable foods did not exist locally as the rebels had burned every farm in the area. As he ate his bacon he was glad he was not a farmer.

3
RECONNAISSANCE

Lt. Malcolm Parker of the United States Army Signal Corps hated the South. He didn't necessarily hate the Confederacy, but he hated the South. His mother was from Louisiana. The bugs, those horrible bugs still haunted his dreams. When his father died they'd moved from Colorado back home as his mother lacked the finances to support him and his two sisters. Where Colorado had been cool in May and the streams full of trout, here it was already sweltering and the river contained strange fish like catfish. When he came of age he headed north to the Rocky Mountains and vowed never to return. Disliking starvation and unable to find much work, he joined the army. And they did not care about his vow to never return to the South.

Then there was the mold and fungus. Something was growing on parts of his uniform. And there seemed no way to get rid of it. He was boiling his uniforms and his Acme Union suit to get rid of it. Nobody told him the little building behind the infirmary was slated for nurses' quarters. He found it had a stove. He found a kettle and decided he'd boil the damned fungus to death.

So, as he sat there watching his uniform cook away, wearing only his birthday suit, the last thing on his mind was that the door would open and three nurses would walk in. He stood out of habit, then thought better of it. They were giggling. He hoped it was giggling, as opposed to outright laughter. He was at a loss for how to explain his situation. "Uh." No words could form in his mouth.

"Are you so hungry you're cooking your uniform?" the pretty blond nurse asked him.

"Un, no ma'am. My uniform has become contaminated by some horrible type of mold that is consuming it."

"I see." She looked over the cooking uniforms, then looked him over. "Ladies, what should we do with him?"

"We could come back later."

"Well, it will take some time for his uniforms to cool and dry. And I am tired." She laid down on one of the bunk beds. "I am not going anywhere. Do you have a name, soldier?"

"Lt. Malcolm Parker."

"Well, Lt. Malcolm Parker, I'm Kevin. This is Hope and that's Sarah. We're nurses and these are our quarters. May I suggest you drain off your uniforms and hang them up to dry?"

He asked, "Okay. Then what?"

"Then you get in bed with me and hump my brains out."

"Oh my God," Hope said.

"You two can join us. I'm happy to share." Kevin started unfastening her nurse's dress.

Hope and Sarah both left with no further discussion.

Kevin said, "I wonder where they're going. I'd think they'd at least want to stay and watch."

This woman was hotter than New Orleans on the Fourth of July and he had nowhere else to go until his uniforms dried anyway. He hurried to get his clothes hung up. She made no effort to help him.

He was asleep. At least he thought he was asleep. There was a smoking hot woman lying next to him, her head on his shoulder. As he stroked her hair he wondered if he was asleep, dreaming, or actually awake and there really was a woman in bed with him.

Apparently, she was not asleep. "Have they invented wireless yet?"

"Wireless?"

"Scientists think it's possible to transmit messages over the air—without the need for wires. I was wondering if they had perfected that yet?"

"What? Why would I know that?"

"Your insignia on the table. That's what signal corps does isn't it, send messages and maintain telegraph wires so Mr. Lincoln can stay informed?"

"Uh." He wondered if she might be a spy. Seduce some naive guy like himself and then pump him for information. "Why do you ask?"

"Oh, I was thinking about building one. It wouldn't be hard. I've just got to get the parts."

"Can't help you there. This supply problem is so bad I can't even maintain our current setup." He was very uncomfortable that a nurse would know about wireless telegraphs, which were being worked on experimentally. He'd seen a demonstration. The prototype had failed miserably and clearly needed a lot more work. He thought a different frequency might help, but the officers running the proving ground didn't care about his shorter wave theory and transferred him to a combat support unit. In the South. Well, he was the one lying in bed with a smoking hot woman—not them.

It grew dark. Kevin made no effort to turn the coal oil lamp on. The door opened and Hope and Sarah returned. Sarah had black hair. Hope, well he wasn't sure what it was. There were streaks of gray and brown.

"Is that man still here?" Sarah asked.

"He is."

Hope lit the lantern. "They're having something called meat pie if you want any. I didn't care for it."

"I'll pass," Kevin said. "You can have a roll with Malcolm here. He's a very good lay."

"You seem happy."

"I'm satisfied. Anyway, I got him to perform oral sex on me. He's a quick learner. You should try him."

"You mean that French stuff?"

"Oui."

Sarah gasped and her face blushed deep red. "I think Malcolm needs to go home now."

He crawled out of bed. His clothes were damp. That would have to do. He headed back for his tent. He'd killed his entire day off boiling his uniform. At least there was no sign of any mold.

He noticed a strange wagon parked next to his tent. There was a woman sleeping on top of it. "Miss, are you okay?"

"Uh, who are you?"

"Lt. Malcolm Parker. I live in the tent here."

"Oh. I'm Mabel, Mabel Saunders."

She was strikingly pretty—even in the moonlight. Even

compared to Kevin. "I don't mean to stare, but you are a strikingly beautiful woman."

"Well, don't tell my sister that. She likes to think she's the pretty one."

"What's her name?"

"You going to go and compare us?"

"She's here? In the camp?"

"She's a nurse. Her name's Kevin."

"Oh. I met her already."

"Did she try and seduce you yet?"

"Uh."

Mabel climbed down from the wagon. "Don't worry about it. We share." She slid her hand down his trousers. "I hope I didn't embarrass you, Malcolm. It's just … well I'd sure like to have a cuddle."

"Your sister wore me out."

"Did she get you to perform oral sex on her?"

"Uh."

"You're kind of shy, aren't you? Let's go get in bed and you can show me what disgusting things you did to my sister."

"Okay."

4
HAPPY DAYS

Kevin opened the door as quietly as she could. She just made it to her bed.

"Where have you been?" Hope asked.

"I just went for a walk."

"It's dangerous out there. Those sentries are ordered to shoot to kill."

"Most of them are still boys."

"Boys with guns."

"And so lonely. They just want someone to talk to," Kevin said.

"Can you two shut the hell up?" Sarah asked.

Kevin finished undressing. She liked sleeping nude. She was sure her roommates wore frumpy nightgowns. She wanted to go skinny dipping in the Mississippi. None of the boys would take her up on that. She must be losing her touch. Getting shot by snipers seemed more important than getting laid, apparently. She'd have to try the rebel soldiers and see if they'd go swimming with her.

Finally, the sun came up. Hope and Sarah ran off to grab a biscuit and some bacon before the start of their nursing shifts. Kevin looked at her dress. Miraculously, the blood was only on the apron. She could boil that clean in no time. It was hard butchering the sentries at night.

The rebels were worse than the Yankees. They had shadow sentries to keep the regular sentries from deserting. Problem was, no one was watching the shadow sentries. And it was hard to keep them from crying out.

And butchering them in the moonlight? That was tough. But she was getting good at it. She hadn't butchered men since the Roman centurions. There, she always went for the centurions because they had the shiny helmets. Kevin was not sure why she liked the sentries. The sleeping soldiers would be easier to butcher. And the cooks were always amazed that she

could come up with fresh pork and they didn't have to butcher
it.

On her way back from the night shift she noticed a young
boy, perhaps four years old, was holding a pig on a leash. "Is
that your piggy?" she asked him.

He shook his head. "Yes," he said, barely audible.

"They burned our farm," a woman said. "I'd a thunk these
Yankees would be doing it, but it was our own." She patted
the boy on the head. "I was hoping we could trade the pig for
transportation to Memphis. I got kin there."

Some major showed up. "Sorry ma'am. We just don't have
anything going to Memphis."

"Sorry Jimmy. I guess our only choice now is to butcher
piggy and hope someone buys the parts."

"No problem there." Kevin grabbed the pig and snapped
its neck. "Anyone got a knife?"

Malcolm was fifteen minutes late to work the next morning.
The major did not seem happy about it. Until the previous
night, his sole sexual experience had been a hand job by Mary
Lou Parker during a picnic at Cherry Creek. Now, well he was
drained but physically there. The major was rattling on about
telegraph lines.

"Parker." That name seemed familiar. It was his. "Yes?"

"I asked you where you think Johnny Reb ran his telegraph
lines."

"I don't know, sir. Few Southern lines are on traditional
telegraph poles. Most run along fence rails."

"Well," he hadn't expected the lieutenant to get that, as
hung over as he seemed to be. "Get your men and find those
damned Confederate telegraph lines. Jeff Davis don't need
to know what's going on here. We don't need them getting
reinforcements. Dismissed."

Not only had he had sex. He'd been the first officer to get
the new Winchester repeaters. He was dying to shoot his, but
they'd been so busy trying to keep the telegraph lines open.
The last outage was caused by a squirrel. Now they had to
bring down the enemy telegraph lines. That wasn't so hard, but
required going into enemy-held country. He did not relish the

thought of going to Andersonville. He'd heard unbelievable things before General Grant suspended the prisoner exchange program. Maybe his new rifle would keep him safe. There weren't going to be any more prisoner releases. Grant was going to starve the South of soldiers.

Mabel took a photograph of two brothers from Arkansas. They were so polite. She framed it up and the boys were so incredibly grateful. She politely declined their marriage proposals and got going in her wagon. She headed away from town, hoping to find some quiet place and take a break from the war.

Only then did she notice that eleven soldiers were nearby. She thought they were cavalry, then decided otherwise. One of the men was climbing up in a Sycamore tree. Two others stood guard with rifles. And they were in blue uniforms—way behind enemy lines.

She headed her wagon toward the soldiers. She recognized Malcolm. These men were Signal Corps. And their world was about to change.

"Lt. There's a Confederate Cavalry troop heading your way," Mabel warned.

"Much obliged."

She pointed behind herself. "They're coming from the south."

A few minutes later the Confederates arrived. A captain tipped his hat. "Ma'am, did you see any Yankee soldiers around here?"

"Why yes I did. There were four of them. They rode off along the river just about five minutes ago."

"Thank you, kindly." He curiously looked at her wagon.

"I'm a photographer. Some day when you have more time, perhaps I can photograph you gentlemen."

"That will be superb." They headed off toward the river.

"Sister is being bad."

"How so? And how long have you been here?" Mabel asked.

"You told them there were four Union soldiers. In fact, there were eleven. Sister told a fib."

"Kevin, I kind of liked Malcolm. He's a nice boy. If they

think there's only four of them, maybe they won't send for reinforcements and they can get away."

"Mabel's got a boyfriend," Kevin taunted.

"You are completely insane. Looking for wild vegetables?"

"Yep. The key to cannibalism is the sell. Spice it up and let them think it's pork and they'll gobble it all up. Tell them it's some sentry and they'll puke their guts out."

"Why do you do this?" Mabel asked.

"I hate seeing food go to waste."

"You are warped, dear."

"I offered to share Malcolm with Hope and Sarah. They didn't want him. But my sister's not too proud to share," Kevin said.

"Look, I've got things to do. There are photographs waiting to be taken."

"Take one of me," Kevin suggested.

"That is forbidden. It's forbidden by God. Forbidden by Nick."

"No one's seen Nick in a year."

"That changes nothing. He'll turn up. He's like that bad penny. No matter how many times you dump it in someone's change, it'll keep coming back to you. Nick's a lot like that."

"Mabel, that makes no sense, whatsoever."

"Look, I tolerate your cannibalism. I don't care if you screw mortals because, frankly, I kind of like that myself. But you scare me. You just don't accept the rule of law, even at some arcane or abstract point," Mabel said.

"I'll be going, sister," Kevin said.

"Please do."

5
FOREIGNERS

As she got farther away from the lines, Mabel found herself in unknown territory. She could hear the artillery, but she could not see the town or any of the battle going on. Then, suddenly, there was silence. The Confederate batteries had stopped. The Union artillery, likewise. That seemed odd. Peace did not just break out. She was certain of that.

She looked up. Way above her was a glowing sphere. She was not sure what size it was. But it seemed to be getting bigger. In other words, it was landing. No wonder the artillery had stopped.

Four little green men climbed out. Mabel looked around. She saw no sign of any soldiers. She rode the wagon over to the sphere. "Are you Martians?" She'd never actually seen one. She could speak their language, as all angels could. She wondered why they had webbed feet—Mars didn't seem to have a surplus of water. Since they were only four feet tall it was hard to feel afraid of them. They wore silver uniforms that did not cover their arms and were cut off at mid leg. It sort if reminded her of British Army summer uniforms in an odd way.

She was informed that they thought she was a woman. *"Well, I take it you have a problem with that?"*

"Women are inferior. It is disgusting to have to speak to one," she was informed by the one who seemed to be in charge.

"What do you want?"

"I am Tang Ulbright and I want a male to discuss surrender terms," their leader said.

"Uh, why do you want to surrender?" she asked.

"You stupid woman, you need to surrender to us."

She noticed that men on horseback were riding up behind them. *"Well, Lt. Malcolm Parker is coming right now, but I'll have to translate. He does not know your language."*

"Little..." the young officer said.

Mabel said, "Yes, they're little green men from Mars.

They're not very nice."

"What do they want?" Malcolm asked.

"Apparently they want you to surrender so they won't invade Earth."

He looked at them, then at the glowing sphere and back at Mabel. "You're serious?"

"Deadly. Look, can you get the artillery to fire on that sphere?" she asked.

"Nope. Too far away and no direct line of sight for a heliograph anyway. Union telegraph lines are miles from here. There's a Confederate line around the corner. We just cut it."

"Splice it back together. Direct the rebel fire on that sphere. Destroy it now," Mabel said.

Malcolm looked at his sergeant. "You heard the lady. Get your map, figure the coordinates and if they ask who you are tell them you're Major Calhoun from the 10th Memphis and there's blue coats down here."

He started fumbling through his saddlebag to find a map. "I don't think there is a tenth Memphis, sir."

"Of course not, but they don't have time to ask around. Do it. The rest of you men, uh take cover."

And the Martians found themselves standing in the road by themselves, feeling a bit confused at where the humans had gone.

Malcolm was surprised at how fast the Confederates got their guns turned around and how accurate they were. One cannonball actually went right through the still-open hatch and exploded inside the craft. When the shooting stopped, there were just three Martians. The fourth one was scattered all over the road.

Mabel told them in Martian, *"You boys might need to rethink your invasion strategy a little."*

"How do we get back to Mars?"

"Well, maybe someone will give you a ride or something." She noticed her sister was sitting on the wagon. "Hey, Kevin."

Kevin yelled, "Wanna do a threesome with Malcolm?"

The young officer started to blush as his men all stared at him in amazement.

Mabel yelled back, "Not right now. Look what we got."

"Martians?" Kevin asked. She'd never really seen one, either.

"They're all yours," Mabel said.

"*Thank you very much.*" the Martian leader said.

Mabel said, "*Oh, you don't need to thank me.* Uh, Malcolm, maybe your men should get going to wherever they go. We'll catch you later."

"Uh, okay." The Union Army Signal Corps became the first earth combat unit to engage in interstellar battle. "Mount up men, let's get out of here."

Commanding General Ulysses S. Grant tapped his fingers on the table. He'd read the report, twice. He took a puff on his cigar. "Uh, Mabel, this is the strangest report I have ever read. You stand by it?"

"Yes, General."

"Lt. Malcolm Parker, do you stand by it?" Grant asked.

"Yes, General."

He took a bite of his lunch. "By the way, tell your sister this alligator is delicious. She has really helped us with provisions. A second sphere apparently took the Martians away. How do I send this to Washington?"

"They'll file it away. Perhaps they'll burn it. But we did our duty and reported it," Malcolm said.

"Fine. Dismissed," Grant said. He took another bite of alligator. "I didn't think they had alligators this far north, It's good, but not quite what I expected."

6
OH, MY!

But there was no second sphere," Malcolm said.

"Take your clothes off," Mabel replied. Her dress fell to the floor.

"But," he pointed at the other nurses.

Mabel glanced over at them. "They can watch. I don't mind."

"Ew." Hope and Sarah bolted out the door.

A minute later, there was a knock. Kevin entered without waiting for anyone to actually answer the door. "Good, I'm not too late."

Mabel said, "Never too late. The general loved the meat you fixed him."

"What was it?" Malcolm asked. "It sure wasn't really alligator. Was it?"

"Of course not," Kevin said. "It was Martian."

"Damn that's disgusting."

"Now lay down on the bed," Kevin said. She grabbed his boots and helped yank them off.

"You just chopped them up and cooked them?"

"I never give out recipes," Kevin explained. "Just think of it as road kill. You don't know what it is, but it's not bad."

"But I do know what it is and that's the problem," Malcolm said. "Alligator was strange enough. Next you'll be telling me the pork we had last week was really Confederate soldiers."

"I would never tell you that," Kevin insisted.

"And I never eat anything she cooks," Mabel added.

"Good advice," Malcolm decided. "Damn good advice."

"Now stop thinking, Malcolm," Kevin suggested. "This will be fun."

7
STRANGERS IN THE NIGHT

Mabel stirred the fire with a stick. It was a clear night. She found herself gazing off at the sky. One point in particular caught her eye—Mars. She couldn't help but wonder what the little green assholes were up to on the red dot in the sky. She wondered what it must be like to be a female Martian. If the pompous males were so arrogant that they didn't even want to speak to a human female, how did they treat their own kind? They certainly didn't take them along in their little flying spheres.

Those thoughts turned to the more immediate. She was being watched. How she longed for a nice quiet night where she could simply relax without having to deal with Martians or soldiers or her nutty sister. But that was not to be. "I can hear you. You might as well come by the fire."

"Then you must have extraordinary hearing," a man said. He moved into the camp. He was dressed as a Confederate officer. "Captain Henry Champagne, ma'am." He took Mabel's hand and kissed it.

"Mabel Saunders."

"A pleasure to meet you," he said.

"What brings you all the way out here, Captain?" Mabel asked.

"I, unfortunately, was separated from my horse this afternoon. My cavalry unit was searching for a union detachment who have been cutting our telegraph lines. Then, well ... my horse threw me. I came to some hours later. By then, my men and my horse were gone."

"Captain, I think that's rather hard to believe," Mabel replied.

"So help me, it is the truth," he insisted. "And of you, madam? Why is a lady such as yourself camping out in the woods by yourself?"

"I'm a photographer. I go where the war takes me."

"The war is hardly out here by this creek," Champagne said.

"It's everywhere. It's soldiers burning a barn while a child clutches her doll and watches. It's a prisoner of war being run through the back by a bayonet. It's a prisoner inside Andersonville trying to catch a rat just to have some food. Oh there's plenty of this war everywhere."

"I stand corrected, then."

"Who are you, really?" Mabel asked.

"I correctly introduced myself," the captain insisted.

"You are either a deserter or an imposter," Mabel said. "The Union troops are not in this area."

"Are you a spy?" he accused.

"Just an observer of things. The Union Signal Corps went north to establish a new telegraph line. So you are not what you claim to be."

"Mighty brave talk for a woman traveling alone." He moved with astonishing speed and tried to grab Mabel. He was shocked at how easily she pinned his arm behind his back and drove him into the dirt with his elbow shattered. His jaw dislocated on impact with the ground.

"I think I've heard of your kind," Mabel said. "You would take advantage of a lone woman to feed on when there is death everywhere. You could take a soldier's life, stab him with a bayonet, and no one would think a second thought."

"But I don't like them. I like pretty girls."

"And being pretty, in your world, carries a heavy price," she said.

"You're awfully strong," he grunted. His body was already trying to mend itself. He needed only to stall for time.

"So are you." She released him. "Why don't you just leave? Go off to whatever rock you hide under and leave me alone."

"It's amazing how often I hear that one. 'I only want to be alone.' It doesn't work for the impala being devoured by a lion and it is not going to work for you sweetheart."

"I gave you a chance to walk away. I'll show you no mercy from this point on. You have disrupted my camp and I will tolerate no more of this," she warned.

"Well you're going to get more," Champagne said. "And that necklace you wear. It looks like a key of some kind."

"What of it?" Mabel asked.

"I thought it was silver, but it's not. I'm free to take it." He reached for it.

She grabbed his hand and snapped back three of his fingers. Each one popped when it broke. "I don't know why you think you can help yourself to whatever does not belong to you. I always thought Southern officers were gentlemen, but you are nothing but a cad." She shattered his wrist.

"What are you? No woman has the kind of strength you possess."

"Apparently you are misinformed, Captain Champagne. Would you like me to break your other arm as well?"

He drew his revolver. Before he could aim it, she grabbed it and took it away from him. Then she snapped his sword right off its belt. "I'm not an expert on this, but I am guessing you don't do too well if you're missing a head."

He stood up. "Whatever you are, I'll find out!" He ran away into the darkness.

Mabel picked up her stick and stirred the coals again. She actually wished her sister had been there. Kevin would have torn the vampire to pieces. Mabel was simply glad he was gone.

The morning sunrise meant it was time to move on in search of new photographs to take.

Reveille starts the day in the army. And it did not matter which army. As the sun's rays came over the horizon a young bugler belted out the traditional tune to awaken the Confederate encampment just ahead of her. There weren't many men, perhaps 200. They were well outside the city and not under the siege. The sentries looked her over suspiciously.

"What is your business here, ma'am?" a young corporal asked.

She explained, "I'm a photographer. I was wondering if some of you gentlemen would like to pose for a photograph."

"Does it hurt?"

"No, Corporal, it does not hurt," she assured him. "You just have to stay put for a couple of minutes. Then it's done."

Few people had seen photographs, let alone been in one. It didn't take the corporal very long to round up a few of his buddies. Mabel arranged them on a wagon. Opened the lens, counted out to thirty and capped the lens. "Okay, gentlemen.

Now it'll take a while to prepare the actual print. I'll come and get you when it's ready."

"Okay Mabel," the corporal said.

8
SPIES

Kevin looked down at the blood on her apron. At least the surgery was over. Doc Clampett held out a pre-rolled cigarette. She shook her head. "Don't care for them."

"I would've sworn I saw you smoke," he said.

"My sister puffs on cigars now and again. Not me."

"The redhead that takes all the pictures?" he asked.

"That's her." The bugler walked by the hospital tent. Kevin asked, "Why do you want to play that thing here?"

"It's kind of an army tradition. It goes back to George Washington during the Revolutionary War."

"Not playing, why do *you* do it? You're not going to be able to hide it forever," Kevin said.

"Hide what?"

"How old are you, 12?" Kevin asked.

"Thirteen."

Kevin moved over to the bugler what's your name?"

"Francis."

"Francis or Frances?" Kevin asked.

"What?"

"'I' for a boy or 'e' for a girl." She moved really close. "I know you're a girl. You're not going to fool these guys much longer." She smiled at Doc Clampett. "Tell her Doc."

"Tell her what. That I know she's a girl. It ain't no business of mine."

"Dang," Frances said.

"How come you're doing this?" Kevin asked.

"I ain't got nowhere to go. They burned down our farm."

"Any family?"

"My pa died the next day. It was just too much for him. Ain't got no kin left. They let me bugle and at least I get fed."

Kevin said, "Well, I suggest you figure something else out. But we won't tell. What do we care? Ain't even our army."

"How come you're here anyhow? Yankee doctor and a

nurse. You do know this is a Confederate camp?"

"We know. There's a Union soldier inside. Had a bullet near the heart and there's no surgeon here. The commanding officer asked General Grant to send one."

"He gonna be okay?" Frances asked.

"With a little luck he may pull through," Doc Clampett predicted.

Frances asked, "How come, if Grant knows we're here, he don't hunt us down?"

"He's too busy trying to force Vicksburg to surrender. This little band of soldiers ain't worth the trouble," she explained.

"Everyone thinks that photography lady is a spy. Guess not if the bluecoats already know we're here," Frances said.

Kevin asked, "Photography lady?"

"Down by the creek."

"Show me."

●

Little sister, you do turn up everywhere," Kevin said. "This is Frances, the bugler."

"Really?" Mabel looked at Frances for a moment. "They let girls bugle?"

Frances asked, "Am I foolin' anyone?"

"Well, not us," Mabel said. "Uh, sis, you do realize we're surrounded by Confederate soldiers, right?"

"It had occurred to me. I better be getting back," Kevin said.

"Back to what?" Mabel asked.

"The hospital tent. That's why we're here. Colonel Ford's shot up pretty bad and they don't have a surgeon to mend him," Kevin explained.

Mabel asked, "What happened to their surgeon?"

"Snakebit," Frances said. "Sat down on a copperhead."

"Well, I've gotta get back," Kevin said. "Take care, sister."

"She really your sister?" Frances asked.

"She really is."

"You go around by yourself taking pictures?"

"Indeed I do."

Frances looked at the other side of the camp. "Gotta play Taps in a bit. Nice meetin' ya."

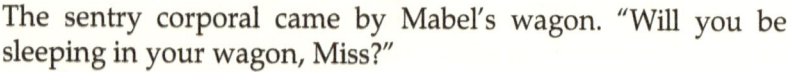

The sentry corporal came by Mabel's wagon. "Will you be sleeping in your wagon, Miss?"

"It's not too bad, really."

"I must warn you, do not leave the area around your wagon until daylight. The sentries will shoot," he warned.

"I understand, Corporal."

"Goodnight, Miss."

"Goodnight, Corporal."

"You staying tonight?" Frances asked.

"Yep, too dangerous to run around at night," Doc Clampett said.

"How come they're letting you help that man?" she asked.

Doc Clampett explained, "You are surrounded by Union troops. A little compassion can't hurt at this point. Besides, I've heard of this before—on both sides."

Kevin found a vacant cot and decided to rest. It had been days since she had any rest. Even with her physiology, she was starting to tire. She also discovered Doc Clampett snored.

After about an hour, something didn't seem right. Something was missing. The bugler was gone. She'd been sitting right next to the tent. It seemed unlikely she'd be wandering around the camp in the dark. That was a good way to get shot.

Kevin set out to search for her. An angel's eyesight was about twice as good as a mortal human. But this was a new moon night and all there was to see by was starlight, and the clouds obstructed a lot of that. Pitch black was the reality and even her vision was limited. She tried to walk as quietly as possible to avoid tangling with the sentries. She could hear a few of them moving around, but could not actually see any of them.

Then she spotted her quarry. Captain Champagne was carrying Frances under his right arm much as a hunter would haul around a poached pheasant.

"Put me down, asshole!" Frances was yelling.

"I should wash your mouth out with soap," the captain said.

"Why don't you wash yours," Kevin suggested. "Or I could

do it for you."

Frances plopped down on the ground. "What is this pervert?"

"He's a vampire. They're vile creatures that drink people's blood. Stay behind me, Frances."

"There aren't a lot of little girls to feed on," he protested. "They're the best."

"And you were told to move on," Kevin said.

"I don't know what you and your sister are, but I've had enough of this." Champagne drew his sword.

"You are most welcome to fall on that," Kevin said. "Let me help!"

He took a swing at her but only came up with air.

Then Captain Champagne yelled out in agony. A piece of wood stuck out of his chest and through his back. "By some damn little girl!"

"Afraid so," Kevin said.

Frances backed away. Her hands were shaking. "I never seen no vampire before. Heard about 'em though. Wood through the heart."

"That's right," Kevin agreed. She picked up his sword and lobbed his head off for good measure. A second later he just sort of turned into dust.

Morning couldn't come quick enough. They loaded their patient on a buckboard at first light. They made it about 300 feet before the camp sentries stopped them. A captain they had not seen the day before looked them over. "Whose idea was this, letting Yankees into our camp?"

"Your colonel," Doc Clampett said. "What's one wounded prisoner going to affect things in this whole giant war?"

"A bullet woulda been easier." He looked over Kevin. "And my men could've ridden you all night long." He shook his head. "No, this ain't right" He dragged Kevin off the buckboard. "Go on, take your wounded soldier. But she stays."

"When General Grant hears about this, I assure you every single one of you will die. Up till now you might've gotten favorable surrender terms. Keep her and that all changes," Doc Clampett warned.

"Go while you still can," the captain warned.

Doc Clampett looked at Kevin.

"Get him back to camp. Go," she said.

He snapped the reins and the horses started moving.

"Second thought." The captain drew his revolver and shot the doctor in the back. Then he went up and shot the wounded prisoner right between the eyes. "You Yankees can all burn in hell!"

He told one of the sentries, "Go and find that other woman, the one who makes the pictures. She was camped down by the creek. We're gonna have some fun, boys."

"That's what you think," Kevin warned. "Big mistake."

The captain slapped her.

"Really big mistake!"

"I'd shoot you if you weren't so pretty."

"Really big mistake."

9
SIEGE

"**Thank you,** Mabel. I'm glad you were able to get out of there," General Grant said.

"And they strut around calling themselves 'gentlemen.'"

"Mabel, war brings out the worst in people. Still, they're surround and outnumbered. I might have even let them surrender their weapons and go home. So few men as that group is of little value. Would've been worth it not to have to fight them. Not now. They've forced my hand."

"I'll stay out of your men's way. Still, I'm sure there would be pictures to take," Mabel said.

"Thank you, Mabel. That will be all," Grant said.

A cavalry officer entered Grant's tent and saluted. "Major Jonathan C. Calhoun of the Kentucky Fifth Regiment reporting as ordered, sir."

"You're familiar with the encampment of around 150 Confederate soldiers five miles north of our camp? Grant asked.

"Yes, sir."

"I want you to back up Colonel Roberts infantry. Leave as soon as you can muster your men. I want this over by tonight."

"Sir, what exactly? We thought they were about to surrender," Calhoun asked.

"Not anymore. Show no quarter. I want no prisoners. Kill everything in that camp whether it's a soldier or their damned commander's dog."

"Yes sir."

"And your unit is going to contain them. No one leaves that camp alive, major. Absolutely no one."

"Yes, General."

"You've got a lot of Southern men in your unit."

"Yes we do. But our state has not left the Union, sir. Nor have we."

"Glad to hear it. Dismissed."

The major saluted and left the tent. A dispatch rider

immediately entered.

Grant accepted a note and looked it over. "No response, Corporal," Grant said. He lit the note from Lt. General John Pemberton, in command of the Confederate forces, on fire with his cigar.

"Sir," the young sergeant saluted, "We can't find any soldiers in this camp—at least not any live ones."

Another soldier dragged up a young boy.

"Excepting him, sir. Appears to be the bugler. Calls himself Francis," the sergeant said.

"What happened here, boy?" Major Calhoun asked.

The boy started crying. "I dunno. I was hid under a wagon."

"Most of them were run through with a bayonet. A few lost their heads to a sword." The sergeant hesitated a moment. "And we found one captain who was shot in the ass, apparently by his own revolver. We also found the bodies of Doc Clampett and the prisoner he came to operate on."

"Everybody in this camp?"

"One hundred sixty-three bodies, sir."

"Unbelievable."

"And one female nurse is missing," the sergeant added.

"What about the boy?"

"Let him go. Go home, kid."

"Ain't got no home."

"Well, go to New Orleans then. There's gotta be work there. You don't want anything to do with a prisoner of war camp." He thought the boy seemed fairly pretty. It had been a really long time since the sergeant had seen his wife. "Get on out of here while you still can."

The sergeant looked around at the bloody carnage. "Looks like they pissed someone else off besides us."

The next morning at 08:00 the dispatch rider arrived with another note from General Pemberton. He opened it. "They surrender."

Mabel poured him some coffee and some for herself. "I'm sure that's a relief."

"We have effectively cut off Arkansas, Louisiana, and Texas

from the rest of the South. This is huge. Maybe Lincoln will shut up and stop wiring me every day with his stupid ideas."

"You were the one that sent out the Signal Corps to keep the telegraph lines working," Mabel pointed out.

"Well, this is one telegram I look forward to sending. Now, what do I do with all those prisoners?" Grant asked.

She stirred the stew around. It needed salt. She had other spices, but not any salt. "This is the most inconvenient war I have ever seen." Hope and Sarah each accepted a bowl. They looked it over, smelled it, then dug in.

"Where do you find meat?" Hope asked.

"You gotta get out there and look for it," Kevin explained.

The door to the nurse's quarters opened up. Mabel entered. "They think you're dead."

"I look dead to you?" Kevin asked.

"Well, I guess not."

"You want some stew, sister?" Kevin asked.

"Uh, no thank you," Mabel decided. "Not really hungry."

10
PURGATORY

June, 1884
San Francisco, California

The men in the Palace Saloon kept trying not to notice her. By that, they didn't want to appear to gawk or leer at her, but she was beautiful. It was impossible to completely fail to discover her. So, fleeting glances were the norm of the day. Except for five men in business suits at the back of the room. They were so busy playing cards they seemed oblivious to her presence. And the cigar smoke was so thick it was possible they couldn't even see her.

But there she sat on a barstool near the front of the saloon. She'd come through the batwing doors just five minutes earlier. It might as well have been an hour. Every man in the room noticed her instantly. Her red and white stripped dress fit her perfectly. The matching hat was beautifully centered over her gorgeous red hair. And those eyes. Every man in the room avoided eye contact. To look into her cobalt blue eyes would certainly mean surrendering your heart to her. Sure, this was San Francisco, not some cow patch on the plains. There were attractive women to be seen. But not this attractive and certainly not in the Palace Saloon.

Couples and ladies simply did not come there. This was a man's bar—a place for drinking and cussing and playing cards. Excepting the saloon girls, but they didn't really count unless you wanted a drink or were so lonely you just wanted somebody to talk to. If you bought the drinks, the saloon girls would talk to you—as simple as it gets.

No, this elegantly dressed woman was out of place and the barkeep knew it. He slid the beer she ordered down the bar. She smiled at him. Maybe he'd scoop out some peanuts into a bowl. Henry rarely bothered, as he simply hated sweeping the husks up off the floor at the end of the day.

"Why thank you, Henry," she said as she extracted a peanut from the bowl.

He'd even wiped the dust off it. "How'd you know my name?"

"You're wearing a name tag."

"Oh."

She was definitely affecting the men in this establishment, and Henry Shamus McGee had no idea what to do about it. But he did look into the massive mirror hanging behind the bar and made sure his hair was properly combed. There was some sort of stain on the sleeve of his shirt. He'd never paid his appearance so much attention.

At the back of the bar one of the five men with cigars tapped out. He grabbed what was left of his mug of beer and wandered away.

"Room for one more?" It was her. No one saw her approach.

The remaining men didn't know what to do. They looked around to see if anyone else was waiting to play. No one was. There was just her, standing there. Finally Simon Tweed, he was sort of the leader of this group, made a gesture toward the empty chair. She immediately seated herself, took a sip from her mug of beer, then smiled. "Is that stud you've been playing?"

"Yes ma'am," Milo Sandeen replied. "We usually play a dollar ante."

She placed a twenty dollar gold piece on the table. "Then buy me in."

Milo pointed around the table. "Simon Tweed, Horst Bentmueller, Sam Nixon and I'm Milo Sandeen. I run the funeral parlor next door."

She seemed to them as if she had an odd accent. Two of them were thinking Paris, the other two would have guessed she came from New Orleans. All of them were wrong. Very wrong.

"Well, let's hope I don't need your services, Mr. Sandeen." She smiled. "Mabel, Mabel Saunders. A pleasure to meet you gentlemen. Who's dealing?"

The barkeep noticed this woman was not drinking. Oh, she'd purchased a mug, sure enough. And she would take a sip out of it now and again—but only a sip. After an hour in the establishment she still had a nearly full mug. A female card sharp at work? He'd never seen that before. Whatever she was up to would have to reveal itself in its own time. But, where did she come from? You remember a woman like that. And why this saloon?

Milo Sandeen handed Horst Bentmueller a cigar.

"Aren't you going to offer me one?" Mabel asked.

Milo shrugged and handed her one.

She smelled it. "You have good taste, Mr. Sandeen. A Cuban." She slowly licked the outer layer cigar leaf. Licking cigars before lighting was a common practice. Watching her do it, the slow way her tongue glided over the cigar, every man at the table was feeling a tension in his trousers. She finally struck a match and lit the cigar and play resumed.

"Miss Saunders, I must say, that's an interesting necklace you're wearing," Milo said as he dealt the next round. "Is that a key of some kind?"

"Well, sort of."

"That color ... at first I thought it silver, now I am not so certain."

She touched her necklace for a moment. "Platinum."

"What's platinum?" Horst asked.

"A rare metal," Milo answered. "You don't see it too often here. It's gold and silver in these parts—mostly gold."

About then, a well dressed man came through the batwings. Unlike Mabel, no one paid him any mind. No one except Mabel.

"Oh, pooh," Mabel said. "Gentlemen, I fold. We'll have to take this up some other time." She collected her winnings—the vast sum of two dollars—and sat herself back down at a vacant table.

The new arrival quickly joined her. She stared at him and puffed her cigar.

"What are you doing here?" he demanded.

"I said I'd get it back." She opened her purse and nonchalantly handed him a revolver. "And here it is. I'm sorry I took it. The devil's gun. The gun that never misses."

Nick frowned in disgust. "You won it back two days ago at another saloon. Why are you still here?"

She explained, "I wanted to see Miles."

"How do you see Miles by playing poker? Miles doesn't gamble."

"Miles isn't home. The lady at his rooming house doesn't know where he is. Paul's still in his barn. He doesn't know where Miles is, either. I was just killing time, hoping he'd show up."

"Paul is a horse."

Mabel shrugged. "I know he's a horse. And he doesn't know where Miles is. Some Secret Service guys came and they rode off in a wagon."

"The lady who runs that place knew they were Secret Service?"

"No, Paul did."

"Paul's a horse."

"I know he's a horse. I can speak horse and so can you, for that matter. Look Nick, you got your gun back. What more do you want?"

"That key around your neck, for starters."

"I'll never give that to you. You could forcibly take it," she said.

"You know I can't do that."

"Well, you are not getting it. It's mine. It was given to me by God Himself and you can't have it."

"What do you need a key to the Gates of Heaven for? Like you're ever going back there. You're persona non grata like the rest of us."

Mabel took a really long puff on her cigar. Then she blew a perfect smoke ring. "It's mine and I'm not handing it over."

"Yet you gamble with my gun."

"They're hardly the same. Besides, a girl needs protection in a city like this one. Riffraff everywhere."

"I think they may need protection from you," Nick said.

Mabel stared at her cigar for a moment. "Well, something has happened to Miles and I'm going to find out what."

Nick stood, took a drink from her beer mug and said, "Kind of flat."

Mabel said, "I most certainly am not."

"The beer. I don't know what to do with you. You're always running around Earth. Okay, see Miles. Then get back to hell where you belong." He turned and left through the batwings

Mabel leaned back in her chair and puffed on her cigar for a few minutes. Then she snuffed the cigar out and headed outside. She wondered if Nick could play poker. She'd never seen it—not ever. Nor had she seen him engage in any game of chance. Nick was too smart for that. He understood probabilities and such. Where Nick viewed gaming as a way to take advantage of someone, Mabel thought of it more in terms of recreation. The helpless men, desiring her yet unable to quench those desires in a public room. And the desperate. The greedy. They were what made gambling fun—the people, not the odds of payout. The payout, that was almost irrelevant. She was nothing like Nick. For some reason, he was oblivious to that fact.

"Now, where is Miles?"

11
WHERE IS MILES?

She handed Paul a carrot. "Paul, I can't figure out what happened to Miles. Does Mrs. Wilson feed you when he's gone?"

As if to answer her, the door to the little barn behind the rooming house opened. Mrs. Wilson came in carrying a bag of oats.

"Hi, Mrs. Wilson. You may not remember me. I'm a friend of Miles."

"Nadine, isn't it?"

"Mabel."

"Oh, that's right. Miles isn't home."

"I know. I just wanted to give Paul a carrot. He's a magnificent horse," Mabel said. "Oh, he loves oats, too." Mabel helped Mrs. Wilson adjust Paul's feed bag.

"Well, I best be going," Mabel said.

"Miles is a government man. Works for the United States Treasury. He's gone a lot of the time," Mrs. Wilson said.

"I know. Nice seeing you again." Mabel headed for the Claremont Hotel. It was a nice establishment, but not as snooty as the places on Nob Hill. It wasn't a matter of money, really. Mabel just didn't want to be too pretentious or to call too much attention to herself. She could come and go at a place like the Claremont and attract little notice, relatively speaking for a stunning redhead. Price was not really a concern since she made her own money. She could play poker with her counterfeit money, but she would never actually cheat at cards. The difference was a subtle one that baffled Nick, but made perfect sense to her.

Her blue dress was hardly her favorite. But the Wing Chinese laundry had not returned her other clothes yet. The red dress stunk of cigars. There were two problems with the blue dress. There was no matching hat. None of her hats matched it. Secondly, she always remembered a poem she'd once heard warning about the devil with a blue dress on—a poem about some treacherous woman up to no good. It hit a little too close to home.

The blue dress would have to do. She made her way to the Pacific Café. It was where all the Treasury people ate. It was just around the corner from the Pacific Stock Exchange. If she were a spy, that could be useful. In her case, the information was simply expedient. She slid into the booth, opposite a fellow who was eating the ham special as he read the evening edition of the San Francisco *Examiner*. He wore spectacles and seemed about thirty, although he appeared to be losing his hair and his age was hard to tell for certain.

"May I help you?" he asked.

"Hi, I'm Mabel."

"So you are? What can I do for you?"

"Is Wentwoth your first name or your last?" she asked.

"My last. You seem to have me at the disadvantage."

"Where is Miles?"

"Who?"

"Special Agent Miles O'Malley. Where is he, Wentworth?"

"I don't know who you're talking about."

"You guys really put the secret in the Secret Service. You can tell me." For some reason, her usual hypnotic techniques were not working. She was losing her touch.

"Miss, perhaps you should leave." Wentworth seemed to be turning a different color—sort of a purple. "You really need to leave."

"What's your price, then? All I want is to know where Miles is. He left in a wagon with some other Secret Service people and disappeared."

"How do you know they were Secret Service?"

"Paul, his horse, told me. He's mad he didn't get to go."

"Madam, I guess I'm going to have to summon the police to get rid of you," Wentworth proclaimed.

"I'll leave, Wentworth."

"If you find him, say hello to President Grant. Tell him Wentworth sends his regards."

"Wentworth, I hope you know that General Grant is no longer president."

"Of course I know that. And I know he's not in New York writing his memoir, either," he said. "It's hard to get to Deadwood. Trains, then a stage, washed out roads, shit everywhere."

Mabel asked, "He's in Deadwood?"

"I never said that," Wentworth insisted. "Safe journey, Miss Saunders."

"I never told you my last name," Mabel pointed out.

"I never said you did." He looked back at his newspaper. "It says here, on page 23, the last ferry to Oakland is in a half hour."

The train headed out of Oakland. She was not on it. Mabel packed up her belongings, settled her bill with some of her counterfeit money, then snapped her fingers. Seconds later, a ball of fire burst open on the streets of Deadwood. Then Mabel emerged. The first thing she noticed was poop everywhere. Horses going back and forth all day over muddy streets. It was a disgusting muddy soup of poop, flies, mud, and more poop.

And her real last name was not Saunders, but that's the one she used of late—since she met Miles. Truth was, she did not have a last name. Saunders was on a Civil War tombstone. She couldn't just register in a hotel as Mabel. For some reason they always wanted a last name. And this Miss thing bothered her too. Why would anyone want to get married? When in Rome, she'd remind herself. Maybe she'd try being a Mrs sometime. Maybe not.

Then some toothless, bearded guy approached her. "Ma'am, care to buy me a drink?"

Pow. He was out cold.

The local hotel certainly was not the Claremont. It had walls and a bed. That's where the similarity ended. The Chinese laundry had done a very good job of cleaning her dresses. San Francisco was the best. They had the best food, the best clothes, the best hotels. Then there was this place. No one was likely to carry her suitcase. Probably shouldn't have clobbered the town drunk so fast.

She checked in. Mabel looked out the window. That toothless bum was looking up at her. He waved. She moved back away from the window. She plopped herself down on the only chair in the room and looked at her revolver. It was so nice and shiny. It just glistened. She couldn't believe she'd been able to lift it off of Nick. He was probably furious. Then he was always furious. He never seemed happy. A girl had to have protection and this gun could provide it. She slipped it into her purse. Miles had one of these. Nick didn't go around trying to get it back from him. Heck, he actually had given it to him and Nick never gave anyone anything.

Time for some poker. The Silver Dollar Saloon was just across the street. She made it twenty feet before that bum approached her.

"How about we get a drink together?" the reprobate asked.

"How about no."

"Why don't women like me?"

Mabel took a breath to give her a moment to accept the fact this guy was serious. "You're filthy. You have the breath of a sewer. Your clothes are covered in horse shit. You don't even have any shoes on. Are you serious? You really think I want to have a drink with someone like you?"

"Well, if you change your mind, name's Moses. If I ain't passed out drunk I sleep over in a shack behind the livery stable. I'm easy to find."

"Well, Moses, you have a nice day." She headed for the Silver Dollar Saloon. Somehow, she just didn't feel like punching him again. Knocking people out cold was not as rewarding as it once was.

She entered the establishment. There were four card games going on. At least the place had a piano player. You could tell a classy place from a not so classy place by whether they had a piano player. That was one of the Mabel Rules. Nick always thought the Mabel Rules were stupid. She had to do something until President Grant and Miles arrived. It might as well be poker.

One of those card games was faro, which is played against a dealer. And the dealers were usually women. Especially in a mining town, lonely miners were more likely to play faro with a woman dealing—particularly an attractive one. The blond dealer with a British accent was too much competition. Besides, she liked poker better. Three poker games running, all men. And one table only had three players at the moment. That should have been a warning.

"Gentlemen, room for one more?" she asked.

The men looked at each other. One of them shrugged. "Have a seat, Miss. Seven card stud, quarter ante. I'm Seth Bullock, the town marshal, and that's why there's only three of us playing. For some reason, people don't want to play cards with me."

"Because you're a lawman?"

"Well, either that or I'm a really good player."

"I hope it's because you're a lawman. I'm Mabel."

"This here's Tom and Buck."

The saloon girl came over.

"I'd like a mug of beer, please."

"Most ladies want wine," Seth observed.

"Most ladies don't play poker."

"Point taken. Buck, you're dealing."

"Seth, can I bum a cigar off you?" Tom asked. "Seem to have left mine at home."

Seth reached inside his vest and extracted a cigar. He tossed it across the table.

"You didn't offer me one," Mabel protested.

Seth shrugged, then handed her a cigar.

These were not Cuban cigars like they had in San Francisco. If she had to guess, they probably came from some dreadful place like Texas or maybe even Mexico. While she was licking her cigar, every man in the saloon sort of forgot whatever it was he was doing. Card play resumed after she completed her task and lit up.

"I don't recall seeing you around here before," Seth said. "Of course I'm new here myself."

"Just arrived. I'm meeting President Grant tomorrow."

"He's coming here?" Seth was shocked a former president was coming to Deadwood and he hadn't been told.

"Afraid so," Mabel insisted. "Let's play cards."

"Let's."

Two hours later, Mabel finished the beer. She couldn't believe she'd gambled away Nick's gun again. No wonder no one played with Seth. That man was good. But it was simply unethical to use her powers to win at poker. Sure, she could hypnotize the lot of them. She could often tell what a man was thinking. On a good day, she could even tell what a woman was thinking. But, cheating at poker, that just was unthinkable. Mabel may have been cast out of heaven. She might very well be the worst angel there ever was. But she just couldn't bring herself to cheat at cards. Even she had ethical standards.

The gun was gone. The hundred dollars in counterfeit money was gone. Miles didn't understand how she could play cards with counterfeit money and that was okay, but cheating was not. Miles worked for the Treasury Department. They had strange ideas about counterfeiting. Money was too hard to come by. It was easier to just make it. Surely Miles could understand that, but he didn't seem to.

She stepped two feet out into the street.

"Hell spawn!"

Her bad luck was extending way beyond cards. Should definitely burn the blue dress.

"Hell spawn!" the Reverend Henry Bartholomew Blackwell was screaming. And he was pointing right at her. "That thing is a demon from hell."

Definitely should not have worn the blue dress. If she still had the gun, she'd have challenged him to a duel. She turned toward him. Being called a demon, a lowlife creepy demon. Damn. These were fighting words to Mabel. A lowly demon. She was an angel, albeit a fallen one, but an angel still the same. A demon would have killed this man already. And a demon certainly did not look like Mabel. This ignorant man needed to learn the difference. "Sir, and I use that term with hesitation, I do not know what you are carrying on about. But I suggest you go home."

"Demon! Hell spawn!" He pointed a quivering finger at her. "You'll see."

"You are remarkably ignorant. Just because a person lives in hell doesn't mean they're a bad person." The thing bothering her the most wasn't being called a demon, it was how he knew she was from hell. Mortals, they lacked that ability as a general rule. How she missed that gun.

"Reverend, stop making an ass out of yourself!" It was

Seth. "You seem to think everyone in town is a demon or devil or something. Now go home or I'm going to run you in."

"Don't be taken in by the likes of her. The devil has a pretty face."

Now she was being compared to Nick. And Nick did have a pretty face, sort of. And this guy did not know crap about her. She should've just punched him out and been done with it. Boy would he have been surprised if that happened.

So she returned to the hotel. She'd lost at poker and been insulted. She had half a mind to pack up and leave and go back to hell. But that wouldn't explain why Miles was coming to Deadwood. It was such a horrible place. Everything smelled like shit. Why couldn't all the criminals stay in San Francisco so Miles could simply arrest them there?

It was at times like this that she wished Miles still worked as a barber. Sure, he was a terrible barber, but he was always home at night, well almost always, except when she wanted him to do something for her.

12
VALOR

"I'm still here."

Mabel wondered why the hotel didn't have a dining room. Black Hills Café seemed okay, but it was outside and down the street. Where the bum was.

"I dreamed about you last night. I liked watching you sleep," Moses said.

"You dreamed about watching me sleep?"

"That's right."

"Get away from me." She was going to throw at rock at him, but decided not to. She was much stronger than a mortal girl and could easily kill him. Not that killing him was necessarily bad, just more likely to cause trouble.

About then, the stage rolled in. It was early. So much for breakfast. An angel could go a decade without eating, so it was just as well. A familiar form climbed down from the stage. "Hi, General. Long time."

He turned around. "Mabel?"

"It's me." She hugged him. "What brings you to Deadwood?"

"We should go somewhere a little more private," Grant said.

"No problem." Mabel guided him back to her room.

"I asked for the cavalry. They couldn't spare any. I wired the Treasury Secretary and asked for the best from the Secret Service. They said I could have O'Malley from San Francisco."

"The eastbound stage gets in here in about an hour," she informed him. "Hopefully, he'll be on it. But what's going on, General?"

"I was visiting Ft. Dempsey, just east of here a ways. And one of our Crow scouts came in with a message pinned to his shirt."

"Why'd they pin a message to his shirt?" Mabel asked.

Grant gave her a puzzled, sort of annoyed look. "Because he was dead. The Crow and the Sioux, well they're

46

not exactly friends."

"Oh."

"The note said they'd captured a Martian in the Black Hills and were holding him for ransom."

"Oh."

"And I asked the cavalry to come with me. They wouldn't. Might be an uprising. Then I wired Washington and they're sending O'Malley. Not much of a response, if you ask me. If I was still president..." Grant's thoughts sort of faded away for a moment.

"Well, while you're waiting for Miles, I've got business to attend to," Mabel said. She proceeded over to the town marshal's office, where one Seth Bullock was sipping on a cup of coffee. Mabel noticed he was drinking from those blue specked coffee cups that seemed just about everywhere in the western United States. She wondered who made them.

Seth looked up from whatever it was he was reading. "Miss Mabel?"

"I was wondering if I could buy back my pistol from you." The weapon was hanging on a peg directly behind the marshal's desk. And she now had the rest of her counterfeit money from her suitcase.

"It's a fine weapon. But I won it fair and square. I think I'll keep it," he decided.

"I'd give you a hundred dollars for it. That's way more than you gave me for it last night."

"No, I'll keep it," Seth insisted.

"Two hundred." That was all the counterfeit money she had left.

"No."

Mabel moved closer to the desk. "What if I sucked your pecker for you?"

Seth sort of chocked on his coffee. "I'm a married man."

"Really? Where's your wife?"

"Down in Salt Lake City, waiting to see if things work out here before moving. This town's still grieving over Wild Bill. Those are some pretty big shoes to fill."

"Well, it's your loss. I could've made you a very happy man."

"Perhaps you best be going, madam."

"Perhaps so," she agreed.

The eastbound stage was rolling in. Mabel ran over to the depot. Miles was the only one on it. She grabbed him and hugged him the second he was out the door,

"Uh, I wasn't expecting you," he said.

"You just disappeared in San Francisco. I tracked you down here."

Miles picked up his suitcase after the driver tossed it down. "I'm on a really secret mission."

"I know all about it." She took his hand. "Come on."

"Not now, I'm tired and I've got things I have to do," he pleaded.

"No, silly. Not that. I want to take you to meet General Grant."

"You know him?" Miles asked.

"Oh, we go way back to the Civil War."

"Of course you do. How silly of me." Mabel was everywhere

"It's not like you and me. I sat with his wife on the platform during his inauguration. Like I said, we're old friends."

And they found the eighteenth president of the United State standing outside the livery stable. Curtis, the livery boy, was explaining, "We just have this buckboard. These are wagon horses, they've never been ridden."

"My hemorrhoids are not going to tolerate some roughshod ride in this wagon, son."

"General, this is Miles O'Malley," Mabel introduced them.

Grant looked him over. "Hmpf. You know why we're here?"

"Doesn't seem like a Secret Service matter. Indians are an army problem," Miles said.

"Young man, everything that goes wrong in this country is a Secret Service problem. Besides, the army is afraid to leave their barracks. Not like when I ran things," He climbed up on the buckboard. Miles offered his hand to help Mabel climb up, although it was doubtful she needed anyone's help. Miles parked himself in back. Buckboards were a lot rougher riding than carriages or buggies.

"Frankly, sir, I don't think the Treasury Secretary believes your story," Miles said.

"Young man, somehow, after you leave the White House, everyone thinks you're an idiot or a kook. After the army wouldn't help, I figured I'd be lucky to get any help at all. But, I just couldn't let this go. The Sioux claim to have a Martian prisoner. I know everyone thinks I'm some crazy old drunk looking for some sort of final glory. It's not like that. Martians. I can't pass this up."

"Fair enough, sir." Miles switched holsters from an inside shoulder holster to an outside model. He noticed Mabel was staring at his revolver. "What? You've seen this before?"

"Its twin is in Marshal Bullock's office in town," she explained. "When we get this over with, can you try and get it back for me?"

"I'll try. Wasn't that ... oh."

"Goodie."

"Mabel, I'm not so sure bringing you along is such a good idea. Miles here is used to dangerous assignments," Grant said.

"I can take care of myself, General."

"Well, open up my case here," Grant pointed at a large carpet bag, "and put together my Sharps rifle."

"You've got a Sharps. They're good guns." She opened the case and removed the parts. She had it assembled in just a couple of minutes.

"They're heavy to carry around, but a damned fine rifle," Grant said. He pulled a cigar out of his pocket. "These things are killing me."

"Can I have one?" Mabel asked.

Grant shrugged, then handed her one of his stogies.

Miles had never seen a woman smoke a cigar. What really caught his attention was watching her lick the darned thing. He'd never forget that moment as long as he lived and it would inspire certain fantasies for the rest of his life as well.

Grant, on the other hand, seemed oblivious to what Mabel did with the cigar before lighting it. He just puffed away on his own cigar as he drove the buckboard.

Mabel coughed a few times. "Where do you get your cigars, General?"

"From some place in Brooklyn. They import them from Haiti or somewhere. They sure are cheap. Helluva deal."

"They're horrible," Mabel said. That didn't stop her from smoking it, however.

No one liked riding in the buckboard. Miles missed his horse. Grant's rear end hurt. And Mabel, she'd never ridden in one before and vowed never to do so again. This was certainly no chariot.

13
INJUNS

About two hours out of Deadwood, Miles declared, "We're being watched."

"Of course we are, silly. The Lakota have been running parallel to us for about an hour now," Mabel said.

Miles asked, "Did you know that, General?"

"Yep."

Mabel added, "Miles, this is a good thing. They want to negotiate over this Martian. We would expect them to be looking us over. If they intended to attack us they'd have already done it."

"Oh." He was so confused. This wasn't a Secret Service assignment, but toss in some Martian and send out the Secret Service because the federal marshals were all a bunch of drunks, the army hides in their barracks and there's no one else left. And how Mabel was involved, well who knew.

The wagon rounded a bend and there were ten Lakota warriors on horseback blocking the road. Grant pulled on the reins and stopped the wagon. "It would appear we have arrived."

One of the Lakota warriors rode up next to the wagon and looked them over. The rest of them stayed back and kept their rifles ready.

"Tell Chief Rain-in-the-Face that President Ulysses S. Grant has arrived as requested. And I hope at least one of you people speaks English."

"Oh we speak English, good," one of them said with a hint of sarcasm in his voice. "Follow."

They were taken to the Indian camp about a mile away. The three of them were seated next to a campfire. "Now they have four hostages," Miles grumbled his unhappiness with the situation.

"Someone's wearing his grumpy face," Mabel said.

"What? What does that even mean?"

"You two act like you're married," Grant observed. "The Indians want something. As long as they think we can get it for them we'll be fine."

"We can't get it for them," Miles said. "That's the problem."

Chief Rain-in-the Face soon emerged from a teepee along with a small entourage of six tribal elders. He looked them over, then sat on the opposite side of the fire.

"I'm President Ulysses S. Grant. This is Agent O'Malley and Mabel Saunders," Grant said.

The chief said something in the Lakota tongue. One of the other Indians translated. "He wants to know why you brought a woman with you."

Without waiting for Grant, Mabel spoke in Lakota. Then she said in English, "I told them I came to translate."

"The chief again spoke. Then the translator said, "We do not need her."

Mabel again spoke, then said in English, "I told them I speak Martian."

"She never fails to amaze me," Grant said.

That revelation got the interest of the Indians. They spoke amongst themselves for a moment. The chief stood. "Come."

The teepee was very dark. All you could see were those glowing eyes, sort of a greenish golden color. He appeared tied. He seemed like he was green in color. It was hard to tell because of the darkness. The creature was not very big, perhaps four feet tall, but since he was tied and laying on the ground it was hard to tell for certain. He had a silver uniform on, but the pants were short. The webbed feet seemed odd. Everyone talked about the canals on Mars and the lack of surface water.

Mabel pushed one of the Lakota warriors who'd been guarding him out of the way. She spoke a strange language. It had a sort of rhythm to it, almost poetic in nature. Then she turned toward the chief and spoke in Lakota.

The chief nodded and everyone went outside. He motioned for some of the women to bring bowls of stew and some sort of berries over by the fire.

"Well?" Grant asked.

"The Martian wants us all to die. He says more are on the way and we will soon be killed. Oh, and he is insulted they brought in a woman to translate. A charming fellow," Mabel explained after she took a bite of the stew. "This is pretty good," she told the chief's wife.

"What do you want out of this?" Grant asked the chief.

"That horrible town sits on Sioux land. The town called Deadwood. We want it removed and gone."

"That is not going to happen. I know Deadwood was built on Sioux land, but the reality of it is it has grown too much to make it go away now," Grant said.

"We tried to make it go away years ago. The Blue Coats stopped us. At least they are not here now. At least you did not come in your Blue Coat uniform." The chief seemed to be speaking a lot better English than he had at first. "It is late." He pointed at a teepee. "In the morning we will try again and figure out what to do with the green man."

Miles asked, "Chief, this Martian, did he have a ship, a flying machine of some sort?"

"And only we know where it is." He again pointed at the teepee. "Tomorrow."

"I could use some rest," Grant said as he headed off toward the teepee.

Mabel sat by the fire and stirred the coals with a stick. Miles decided to join her.

She said, "There's something calming about a campfire. It warms you, can cook your food. Yet, with a gust of wind, it can become a raging torrent of destruction. Both good and bad, a lot like me."

"How'd you learn Martian?" Miles asked.

"You keep thinking of me like a mortal woman. I may look like one, but I am not. I can speak just about any language. All angels can." She stirred the coals again. "It's strange, Miles. I was cast out of heaven, yet God never took away my powers. You've seen some of what I can do. There are other things. You think the world is a screwy place. Try looking at it from my perspective. And there's a code angels must follow. Even me. For instance, it doesn't say a thing about taking a life, but I absolutely cannot bring the dead back to life. Things like that."

"It's binding on you but they kicked you out?"

"Makes no sense."

Miles started for the teepee. "Well, I guess I'll try and get some sleep. Are you coming?"

"No. It's not sleep you'll be wanting. And you know what a screamer I can be. The general needs his rest. He's such a nice man, a nice man thrust into that awful war. And now his beloved cigars are killing him. He needs his rest. I'll stay out here a while. I don't need to sleep like you do."

Miles asked, "Is he dying?"

"Yes. Cigars won't hurt me, but the cancer in him is rapidly spreading and is almost surely the result of smoking. Don't begrudge him a few sips from his flask. He's in a lot of pain."

"Did he tell you this?"

She shook her head. "Of course not. I told you, I'm not like those flimsy mortal girls."

Miles nodded. "So you keep reminding me. Well, good night, Mabel."

"Good night, Miles."

It was right around sunrise when the screaming started. One of the women had taken food to the two warriors guarding the prisoner. She found them both dead. The prisoner was gone. The two Lakota appeared to have been stabbed.

Miles was hopping along on one foot, trying to get his other boot on, still unclear of what to make of all the commotion. He found Mabel talking to the hysterical woman, trying to both calm her down and get information at the same time.

"The Martian untied himself somehow and grabbed a knife from one of the warriors. He's stronger than he looks. Worse yet, he had a weapon that shot some sort of ray. It was in a box and is gone now. He would appear to have it as well."

"He will try and return to the shiny round ball," Rain-in-the-Face said. "But he is on foot and we have horses."

Grant rode up on the buckboard. "Get in!"

"Might as well," the chief agreed. "You probably can't stay on one of our horses since you all use saddles."

There were eight Lakota warriors on horseback, by Miles's count. Plus the chief and the three of them. Grant had a Sharps rifle. The Martian had a knife and some sort of beam weapon. He wondered who had the advantage.

A blueish beam of light severed the head of one of the

buckboard horses. "Take cover!" Grant yelled.

"Yep, advantage Martians."

"He just made a huge mistake," Grant said as they found refuge behind some large rocks.

"How so?" Miles asked.

"He revealed his position."

The chief patted Grant on the back and signaled his men where he wanted them.

"This guy's pretty good," Grant said. "Without saying a word, his men can cover anywhere. Could've used him at Shiloh."

Another flash of blue light broke one of the boulders in two.

"I wonder if he has to reload that thing?" Miles asked.

"Who knows?" Grant replied.

"Let's end this," Mabel said. She was aiming the Sharps rifle.

"That's kind of heavy for a woman," Grant said.

With a really annoyed tone in her voice, Mabel said, "I'll manage." She squeezed off a round. A few seconds later the green guy slumped over a rock. "Welcome to Earth."

Two Lakota warriors ran over to the Martian. One of them made a signal and everybody else moved closer. They all stood around staring at a corpse for a moment. Miles picked up the alien weapon.

"Not much ransom in a corpse," Rain-in-the-Face said.

"Afraid not, chief," Grant agreed.

"Good thing we have flying machine," he said. "Corps of Engineers would like to get that." His English sure seemed to be getting better.

"Take us to it, Chief," Grant said.

"The sooner the better," Mabel added.

So they loaded onto the wagon and headed off to find the Martian contraption. "General," Mabel whispered, "there are more Martians on the way. They'll surely find the spaceship."

"And we'll have nothing for ransom," Rain-in-the-Face said from his horse. The chief had remarkable hearing. "It was worth trying."

The object was parked in a gully. It was a sphere with no

visible exterior moving parts. Two Lakota warriors were sitting on it. They had not left with the group.

"Ah, he had guards on it," Grant said.

14
DECISIONS

"**What do you** want to do?" the chief asked. "If more Martians coming, they will take this."

No one had a chance to answer. There was a loud whirring sound and two more silver spheres came out of the sky. "Take cover!" Grant yelled.

The chief yelled something in Lakota. His warriors tossed burning clumps of grass through an opening. Apparently the thing was already full of dry grass. Smoke roared up quickly, providing cover and doing untold damage to the spacecraft at the same time. Then the captured spacecraft started emitting a loud hum.

"I don't like the sound of this. Run!" Miles announced. The blast happened about a second after that. Miles was the closest to the ship. The shockwave picked him up and smashed him into the side of the gully.

Mabel looked at Miles, then at an approaching column of green men wearing silver suits. Blue light beams started slicing through the air. The Indians returned fire with their Winchester repeaters, but they appeared to be outgunned three-to-one. Mabel fired off a round from the Sharps and one of the Martians went down.

The Martians decided to fan out and take cover. Every few seconds, a flash of light was fired off. Few of them hit anything.

Mabel ripped a piece of cloth from her petticoat. She tied it to a stick.

"What are you doing?" the chief asked.

"Since I speak Martian, I guess I better go and see what it's going to take to get us out of this mess."

It was hard to tell, but they mostly seemed to be arguing. Finally, Mabel returned to the group. "They are highly offended at having to negotiate with a woman. They want us to withdraw from the area. They retrieve what's left of the sphere and they will return to Mars."

"We can't win this one," Grant said. "What do you think, Chief?"

The chief signaled his men. They started pulling back.

Mabel went to the gully. "Miles, time to get up."

"Mabel." Grant wanted to stop her, but knew he couldn't.

"Oh crap." Mabel knelt down and checked for a pulse. "Miles, come on now."

"His neck's broke," Grant said. "Do we bury him here or take him back to town? Deadwood has a large cemetery on Mt. Moriah. The place must be a death trap."

Mabel looked over toward the Martian sphere. "No, he'll be fine. Look inside the sphere. We need a box with two green circles on it."

A minute later the chief returned with just such a box. Mabel removed a small cylinder. Red beams of light shined down on Miles's neck. After a couple of minutes, the light changed to green. "There, that's better."

Miles started coughing, then his eyes opened. "What happened?"

Mabel told him, "Miles, we've got to go. Can you walk?"

Mabel and Grant helped him over to the buckboard. They followed the Lakota back to their camp. Everyone sat around the fire for a while. No one spoke.

Finally, Grant said, "Chief, if that little green guy hadn't escaped, and more of them hadn't shown up, what I'm saying is, it was a good plan. Could've worked. You might've gotten something out of the government." He went over to the buckboard. He picked up the Sharps rifle. "Chief, I'd like you to have this."

The chief looked it over and smiled. "Shame there aren't many bison to hunt anymore."

"I couldn't agree more," Grant said.

"Thank you. That, plus the Martian's gold, should help some for our people," Rain-in-the-Face said.

"Gold?" Miles asked

The chief climbed up on his hose. "The yellow metal that drives white men crazy. Why'd you think the Martians came here? They want it too." He nodded and rode off with his men.

Miles managed to get Seth to sell him the gun he'd won

from Mabel in the card game. He checked out of the hotel and waited quietly for the westbound stage. He'd left Grant sleeping in the hotel as they'd just missed the eastbound stage.

Moses approached Miles. "What happened to Mabel?"

"Uh, she had to leave."

Moses said, "Too bad. She was the sort of woman worth getting cleaned up for."

"Yes, yes she was," Miles agreed.

Truth was, she remained on the Sioux reservation. Mabel said it was a temporary thing,

To someone as long-lived as Mabel, Miles was not sure what that meant.

15
ANOTHER DAY

It was daylight. He looked around. She was over sitting in the chair. She was still naked. "What time is it?"

"It's seven o'clock," she replied without looking at the clock on his dresser.

"What are you doing over there?"

"I like watching you sleep," Mabel said. "Mrs. Wilson has breakfast ready. You better get going. We have reservations for supper at seven, so come by the Claremont and get me around six thirty."

"Madam, did it ever occur to you I might already have plans this evening?" Miles asked.

"No it did not. How could you possibly have plans if I'm in town? See ya." She realized she had no clothes on and stopped to put her dress on before leaving Miles's room.

Miles staggered to the dining room. He was so tired. The government needed to stop sending him all over creation. These long trips were exhausting. If only he was not currently one of only three agents for the entire western region. It looked like flapjacks on the plate. He was not sure what the difference between flapjacks and pancakes was, except Mrs. Wilson served blueberries with flapjacks and syrup on pancakes. It was better to simply eat whatever Mrs. Wilson gave him than think much about it.

"You look awful," she said. "Do you want some more coffee?"

"No thanks. I got back late last night. I'm so tired."

As she poured him some coffee, Mrs. Wilson said, "You weren't this tired when you were a barber."

He wanted to laugh. Those were the good old days. He just cut hair and people would threaten to kill him because their haircuts were so awful. The dogs he groomed always liked their haircuts, though.

Mrs. Wilson poured him some more coffee even though

he'd only taken a sip. "What do they have you doing?"

"He would've sworn he said he didn't want any coffee. He stared at his plate. There were more flapjacks. He would have sworn he'd finished them off. "Counterfeit treasury bonds." That was pretty much the cover story no matter what he was really doing.

At some point there weren't any more flapjacks to eat and he staggered back to his room. An odd fantasy had popped into his head. He was in Washington, in the Treasury Building. The Director asked him, "Is it true you have relations with an angel from hell who is one of the biggest counterfeiters in California?"

"Of course not, sir," Miles would say. "She's not always in California." Then he started laughing.

Mrs. Wilson opened his door at the sound of his maniacal laugh, realized he was buck naked, and closed it quickly.

Miles wondered why he was naked. Oh, his jammies and robe were not considered appropriate attire at the treasury office. Wentworth would have a stroke. A proper suit was needed. He was so tired. He fumbled around trying to figure out why his suit was in the closet.

Wentworth unlocked the office door. He was a bit surprised to see the door to the file room was open. "You're not supposed to be in here."

"I know that," Mabel said. "But this is where the files are."

"What are you doing to my files?" Wentworth demanded.

"I'm redacting them."

"You can't do that. Those are official Treasury Department files."

"Of course I can. I just did. You people really should get some better locks on your doors," Mabel said. "The last time I saw you, you let it slip that you knew I travel under the name Mabel Saunders. I can't have that. Well now it's all gone and I'll use another name from now on. Good day, Wentworth."

"Madame, you are under arrest."

"That's ridiculous."

"Don't make me use violence," he threatened.

"Violence can be fun, Wentworth. Have you ever had a dominatrix whip you? I could introduce you to someone."

"What did you do with the files, anyway? You're not carrying them."

Mabel held out her hand. There was a flash and a small flame burned on her hand for a second then went out. "It's sleepy time, Wentworth." She snapped her fingers. Wentworth closed his eyes and sort of slid down to the floor. "Now that's better". She watched him for a moment. "I don't know why I like watching men sleep. You're kind of cute, Wentworth." She kissed him on the cheek.

Miles was a little surprised to find Wentworth asleep on the floor of the file room. That was so unlike him. Miles was kind of envious. He was so tired. But sleeping on the floor next to Wentworth, that would be sort of weird.

He noted a slip of paper sticking out of Wentworth's pocket.

MADAME VERONICA'S HOUSE OF WHIPS AND PLEASURE

751 ½ SANSOME STREET

Well, at least it wasn't an opium parlor in Chinatown. Miles said, "Wentworth you dog, you." He replaced the slip of paper. Miles decided to go back out to the outer office. He relaxed in the swivel chair and started reading the morning *Chronicle*. The big story of the day was about the fireworks factory explosion. He had no idea there had even been a fireworks factory explosion. He would've liked to have seen that. Oddly, although a few workers had minor burns, no one was seriously hurt. Some cat apparently started the blaze by knocking over a kerosene lantern. They kept the cat around because the place had a mouse problem. Well, it didn't any longer.

There was rustling around in the file room, then Wentworth emerged looking somewhat dazed. "What the hell happened? I woke up on the floor."

"I noticed you were sleeping there. Just figured you were tired."

"Agent O'Malley, I don't get tired. I'm with the Treasury Department."

"So am I," Miles replied. "And I'm tired all the time. This constant travel is wearing me out."

"You have been on the road a lot. But, there's no rest for the weary." Wentworth noticed the paper sticking out of his pocket. He looked it over. "What the?"

"What people do in their off hours is no concern of mine," Miles assured him.

"I've never seen this before."

"It's nothing to be embarrassed about. The late Judge Hastings was a big fan of Madame Veronica," Miles said. Madame Veronica was more than happy to untie the judge if Miles needed a search warrant signed.

Wentworth seemed surprised with that revelation. "Really? And I thought I knew what was going on."

"Yep." Miles put down his newspaper. "So, how about I go and ride my horse and you do whatever it is you do, provided you can stay awake long enough to do it?"

"Very well," Wentworth agreed, not wanting news of his sleeping on the job to spread. He'd thought there was a local counterfeiting case he was going to assign Miles to involving some woman who liked hotels, but there was nothing on the clipboard and no file in the file basket. Perhaps he was more tired than he realized. Sleeping in the file room. That was not like him, not at all.

Miles found Paul in his little barn behind the boarding house. "Let's go for a ride."

Paul started shaking his head like he didn't want to go. Then Miles realized there was a shadow on the wall and there was someone behind him. He turned around.

"Hi Miles. It's been a long time."

"Yeah, it has," Miles agreed.

One Nick Mephistopheles, known by the heaven crowd as Lucifer, known as the devil in some circles, was standing right there in Mrs. Wilson's back yard. "Have you seen Mabel?"

"Yes."

"Could you be a little more specific, Miles?"

"I saw her this morning. She's got dinner plans for us this evening. Why?"

"I think she's avoiding me."

"Sorry. Actually, since you're here, I'll be right back." Miles ran off inside the house while Paul seemed uneasy at being left alone with Nick. Miles came running back a few minutes later. "I … well wasn't sure what to do with this." He handed Nick the twin of his own gun. "Marshal Bullock gave it to me before I left Deadwood. I think it belongs to you."

Nick looked over his gun for a moment. "Mabel can't keep her hands off this thing."

"She likes having protection."

Nick laughed. "The mortals need protection from her, not the other way around. She just wants it because it's mine. If I gave it to her, I would almost bet it would sit in a closet someplace."

This time Miles laughed. "What brings you to San Francisco?" Miles knew Nick doesn't just turn up out of the blue without wanting something. He doubted it had much to do with Mabel. Mabel, eventually, would go back to hell. She always did.

"Well, this evening will be fine, actually," Nick decided.

Miles was not all that comfortable with the idea of Nick turning up on his date with Mabel. But Nick was no longer there. "Damn I hate it when he does that," Miles told his horse.

Paul snorted in agreement.

16
ESTABLISHMENTS

"**Oh good,** you're here," Mabel said. "We're going to that seafood place over on Sansome."

"Uh, okay," Miles agreed.

Mabel was wearing a purple dress that had white stripes on it. Of course there was a matching hat as well. As they strolled along, Miles noticed Wentworth coming out of a home. Mabel followed his gaze. "Isn't that Wentworth?" she asked.

Miles seemed a little surprised. "You know him?"

"He doesn't tell me anything. Some public servant." Mabel watched Wentworth walk away in the opposite direction. "Wasn't that Madame Veronica's he just came out of?"

"Uh, well, I think so."

"You naughty boy," Mabel teased.

"No." Miles seemed bothered. He hesitated, then said, "The late Judge Hastings was a big fan of the place. If I needed a court order I sometimes had to go there. He was there every Friday afternoon. Why do you know about that place?"

She stopped walking and turned and pretended to look in the window of the photography shop they were passing. "Look who's going in there."

Miles took a quick glance. "Uh, I can't believe it."

"Well, let's just say it's good to know who is doing what," Mabel said. She started walking again and had to tug Miles along. "Come on."

"But, that was Nick?" Miles seemed confused, even for Miles.

"Miles, I'm a lot older than you. I've learned not to judge people. If someone wants a dominatrix, that's their business," Mabel said. "Although I do like to keep tabs on him in particular."

"Well, you know him better than I do," Miles agreed. "But, Nick, well he came by the house this afternoon. I wasn't sure why."

"I've learned, when it comes to Nick, I can't outguess him.

If he came by to see you, just take it as it is."

Miles shook his head. "He wanted to know what you were up to, not me."

"If we're at dinner, what better time to not have to worry about me finding out he wants to be whipped and tied up. It's just a coincidence he didn't know where we're going to dine this evening."

Miles asked, "You don't seem all that surprised?"

"I've known Madame Veronica for quite a while. She used to be a faro dealer named Peggy Falstaff. Then she discovered certain gentlemen like certain things polite society doesn't quite understand."

"Oh." He opened the door to the restaurant.

"We have a reservation for O'Malley," Mabel told the maitre d'.

"Of course," the tall man wearing a white shirt and a black bow tie said. "Right this way." He guided them to a table by the window with a nice view of San Francisco Bay. He handed them each a menu and said, "Your waiter will be right with you."

"I love San Francisco. Nice views and there isn't poop everywhere," Mabel said.

Miles cringed when he noticed the prices on the menu. Washington would never understand Mabel and her counterfeit money. He was glad he didn't have to explain her.

They both ordered the halibut, which was described as the catch of the day.

"San Francisco's on the ocean," Mabel said.

"I know that. My house is a block from the Pacific Ocean."

"We're having seafood."

"I know that too."

"Don't order seafood in Denver, Miles. Or any landlocked state."

"Uh, that makes sense," he agreed.

The waiter brought them some bread. Mabel took a bite. "I love the bread here. No bread anywhere else in the world tastes like San Francisco sourdough. It's just wonderful."

Miles noticed, as he slapped butter on his bread, that Mabel was eating hers without any. "We always put butter on our bread growing up. It's a habit I can't break."

"Then put butter on it. Eat it the way you like it, Miles. Oh, here comes our meal."

They finished their meal. Mabel paid for it, presumably with her counterfeit money. Miles didn't ask. Then they started back for the hotel.

"Miles, one of the things I like about you is you don't judge people. Take Nick, for example. Now, most people would just go nuts if they knew who he was. Not you. You just treat him like anyone else. And me. Some preacher was talking about me in his sermon last month."

"Wait? You went to church?" The concept seemed very odd to him.

"Sure. I like church. The singing and stuff. Anyway, he was talking about the evil angels God cast out of heaven. Heck, he acted like there was an army of us. There are only four. I had a good mind to take my donation back from the collection plate. He said we were the epitome of evil."

That didn't register right to Miles. "Take back your counterfeit money?"

"Darn tootin'. As I was saying, I didn't care for that."

Miles said, "I didn't even realize there were any angels in hell until I met you."

"Are you glad you met me? Actually, that's an unfair question."

"No, I mean yes, I'm glad I met you. It's been an amazing experience few of us mortals could ever have."

"I hate to change the subject, but those four men coming up behind us are up to no good," Mabel whispered.

Miles spun around toward them and drew his revolver. He noted one of them had a small blackjack, which was a kind of club. One had a dagger. If the other two had weapons, they were not displaying them. "Federal agent! Drop your weapons."

They didn't drop their weapons. They did turn around and run away. One of them dropped something as he fled. Mabel went to retrieve it.

"Decent folks can't go anywhere in this city. I should stop coming here," Mabel said.

"You were just going on about how much you like it here,"

Miles pointed out. He returned his gun to the shoulder holster. "Well, whatever these guys are up to, they're not very good at it."

"They're college kids. I doubt they're used to violence," Mabel said.

"How do you know they're college kids?" Miles asked.

"One freshman beanie, blue and gold. I'd say they came from across the bay at U. C. Berkeley."

"You would've made a good detective," Miles said as he looked the hat over. "So that's what these stupid hats are. I'd always wondered."

"Back when I was teaching at Radcliffe, we just had girls. But the Harvard boys ran around with those stupid hats on. Just one semester." She sounded bitter. "They didn't seem to like my attitudes on things. They said I had loose morals."

"How did you get hired as an instructor?"

"I was a visiting professor. I made up a background and they never checked. Loose morals. I'll never work there again."

"You absolutely never fail to amaze me," Miles said.

"I don't think they were going to rob us."

"I think you're right. Maybe I'll take a trip across the bay tomorrow and see if I can find out anything," Miles said.

"Goodie." They were at the hotel. "Want to come to my room? I'll be your prisoner and you can handcuff and search me."

"Search you for what?"

"Anything you want."

17
THREE A.M.

Mabel opened the door to her hotel room. She was wearing a sheet and nothing else. The bellboy nervously tried to avoid looking at her. "It's three o'clock in the morning. This better be good," she snapped.

"There is a gentleman at the loading dock," the bellboy nervously said.

"Why would I care if there is some gentleman at the loading dock?"

"He wants to talk to you."

"At the loading dock? At three o'clock in the morning?"

"Yes ma'am." The bellboy scampered off as fast as he could move without looking like he was running.

She looked over at Miles, who was sound asleep, buck naked on the bed as she had the sheet wrapped around herself. "Bloody hell." She went down the back stairway in her sheet, wondering if she should have grabbed the gun from her purse. Then she remembered she no longer had one as she'd gambled hers away again. Perhaps she could've borrowed Miles's gun. A man in a top hat at three a.m. at the loading dock of a hotel?

It was no man. He looked sort of like a man at a distance, or in the dark. "Ellul?"

"Mistress Mabel."

"What are you doing here?" Mabel asked.

"Can't find Mister." He couldn't ever pronounce Mephistopheles. "Can't find Mister."

She shrugged and almost lost control of the sheet. "Why tell me? I don't even like him."

"I went to Madame Veronica's. She said he left. She offered to spank me."

"Get to the point. I'm standing here in a sheet and I'm sure not going to spank you."

"Kevin."

Her eyes rolled into the back of her head for just an instant.

She tried to steady her breathing. "You think she's here, in San Francisco?" Mabel asked.

The demon Ellul replied, "That's where the cherubs are. In Golden Gate Park."

"Oh dear. But you found me. Okay, keep looking for Nick. I'll go get some clothes on."

Miles woke up as she was lacing her shoes. "What are you doing in my britches?"

"Something bad has happened. I've got to go." She picked up his gun.

"That's my gun," he protested.

"I know. I've got to go." She bolted out the door. Miles's clothes didn't fit her. They were too big. But it was better to be dressed to look like a man at three o'clock a.m.. If any of San Francisco's finest were awake and sober, it guaranteed a confrontation if she was thought to be a woman running around at that time of the morning.

She found two cherubs, with their little helmets still on, just lying there. They looked like some sort of wild animal had attacked them. In a way, one had. Mabel grabbed each of the collars of what was left of their robes. She was so used to snapping her fingers. She focused her thoughts and willed a fireball to form. "Not even a damned cherub deserves this."

The gate was locked. Of course it was. She remembered the necklace she wore. It was supposed to be shaped like a key to heaven. She took it off her neck and tried it. The gate opened. The two white horses hooked to the chariot were thinking about bolting. "Don't you dare," she warned them. She threw the two cherub bodies into the chariot. "Take them to the palace."

Mabel started for the gate. Someone behind her was yelling. "It's her! That crazy one from hell! She's killed the cherubs!"

"Wonderful." She was almost clear of the gate when a blinding column of light caught up to her.

Mabel knelt and lowered her head. "I couldn't just leave them on Earth."

And this hell spawn hath destroyed my cherubs.

"With all due respect, cherubs have no business on Earth. It is the angels who were born to fight your battles there," Mabel said. "And Kevin was from Heaven, originally—just like me."

Angels seem to struggle when asked to battle other angels.

"Yes, Lord."

Will thou take up this task?

"Yes, Lord."

And God was gone

Mabel crossed the threshold of the gate. The gate closed. She looked back at the horses on the other side. "Why not send me. I am completely expendable. If I end up looking like those cherubs, no one will even care. Good move, God." She snapped her fingers. "Damned good move, even for Him. Get Mabel to do it."

This time thing was annoying. Time passed at a different rate in heaven than it did on earth. It was dark, around midnight. Miles was so cute when he slept. He had an angelic quality—but in a good way. "Miles."

"Whu…"

She gently touched his shoulder. "Miles, I need you to wake up. And don't wake Mrs. Wilson's boarders."

"Whu…"

She took the washing pitcher and made sure that was what it was. He was sore about her dumping the chamber pot on him for a really long time when she last attempted to wake him.

"Yikes."

"I haven't got time. I need to borrow Paul."

"Why have you got my clothes on? I wore a dress home. And Mrs. Wilson saw me in it. She's been giving me funny looks all day."

"Look. I'm borrowing Paul." She held up his gun. "And I'm borrowing your gun. Where are the bullets?"

"It's loaded. Besides, you already took my stuff last night."

"But I didn't ask for it." She opened the chamber and checked the ammunition. "Not these bullets. You used to have titanium bullets. The bullets designed to take down the Titans but they can also kill an angel. I know you lied to Nick and kept some. Give them to me. Now please."

"Dang. I shouldn't be arguing with you. They're my bullets," Miles protested. He took his Sunday shoes out of the closet. He turned one of the shoes over and six shiny bullets dropped out. "That's all there are."

Mabel took them and re-loaded the gun with them. "I've got to go."

"You won't even tell me what's happened?"

"No. It's for your own good," Mabel explained. "There's an angel named Kevin who's causing some problems."

"What's that got to do with you? Doesn't God have an army of flunkies? He can't be that tough."

"She is my sister and yes, she is that tough."

"What's she done?"

"Well, she's long wanted to exterminate mankind, for starters." And she was gone.

"I always thought Kevin was a boy's name. These angels drive me crazy. I was wearing a dress today," he told an empty room. "I was in a blasted dress that didn't even fit. I rode on a cable car in a dress that did not fit. In the rain, no less. Why do I put up with her? And some man kept making kissy faces at me on the cable car."

18
THERE IS NO PIE

The pie was gone. He remembered smelling the apricot pie cooking, except it was probably a cobbler. It would've been packed full of apricots from Mrs. Wilson's trees. And it was all gone. He checked the little shed out back. His horse was gone. He was an unarmed federal lawman with no horse. But at least he had a second suit. Running around the city in a dress was not going to work. What looked good for Mabel did not look quite right on him.

He was pleased to find Mildred's Café was open. "May I have some apricot pie?" he asked.

"No," the pretty blond waitress replied. She must be new. He'd certainly never seen her there before. She had pretty green eyes. She was tallish, but not overly so. "Ain't got none."

"But there's some underneath that cover," Miles protested.

"No there isn't."

"I can see it." He pointed at it. "It's right there."

The waitress opened the top of the display, picked up the pie and threw it into Miles's face. "As you can plainly see, that is a cobbler and you asked for pie, which we do not have."

"And I was obviously in error. Good day madam." He opened the door and departed the establishment. Why had Mrs. Wilson not saved him a piece? Why had the cosmos suddenly turned on him to deprive him of single slice of apricot pie or apricot cobbler? And why had the waitress reacted so violently?

The old Miles O'Malley would have raised a scene; demanded to know why there was pie all over his face and his only remaining suit. He did not care. The new, more fatalistic version of Miles simply headed for the local Chinese laundry, which was closed. Of course they were closed. It was really late at night. Why would the laundry be open at three a.m.? For that matter, why would the café be open?

He started running. The café was closed now. The lamp

was dim. But the front door was not locked. He turned up the light and searched around the establishment. He found a waitress on the floor, her neck appeared to be broken. And it was definitely not the waitress who had thrown pie on him. He opened the door and began yelling for the police.

To his surprise, an officer quickly arrived. "What seems to be the problem, sir?" the policeman asked.

"There's been a murder. The waitress inside is dead," Miles explained.

"And you have pie on your shirt." The policeman drew his gun. "A very interesting coincidence." He started blowing his police whistle.

Miles showed the officer his badge. At least Mabel hadn't run off with that. "I am a United States Treasury Agent."

And, badge and all, Miles found himself in a holding cell. He figured at least three hours had passed as he sat in the cell. At least he was by himself and not sharing with some drunken unfortunate who smelled like poop. There was just himself, who smelled like pie. He wanted out. He wanted desperately to get a clean shirt that did not smell like apricot cobbler. And he wanted to figure out whatever it was that had gotten into Mabel—running off with his gun and his horse and his clothes. That certainly was not like her.

Finally a uniformed officer came and moved him to an interview room. He sat in a chair for five minutes, then a man in a gray suit entered the room. "I am Inspector Hancock."

"Miles O'Malley."

"Mr. O'Malley," he tossed Miles's badge on the table, "is this real?"

"Yes. You can verify it with Wentworth in the federal court house."

"When they open. And this waitress, a blond haired woman with green eyes, threw pie at you?"

"Yes. She became enraged when I referred to the apricot cobbler as pie. Then she threw it on me," Miles explained.

"This café closes at nine o'clock. It was, according to your statement, around two o'clock a.m.. Were you not in the least bit suspicious as to why this establishment was open so late?"

"I was hungry. I didn't get any supper where I live. I didn't think about the time until later. I just wanted some pie."

The inspector wrote something down in his notebook. "And you got some."

Then Miles had to re-state every detail of the previous evening, including the dead waitress and how she was dressed. This went on for another hour. Then the door opened and Wentworth entered. He whispered something to the inspector, then the inspector left.

"Mr. O'Malley," Wentworth said, "how do you manage to get yourself into these situations?"

"It's a gift, Wentworth."

"Well, they said you could leave. Let's get out of here before they change their minds."

"An excellent idea," Miles agreed. When they got back to the treasury office, Miles asked, "Can I get a revolver issued to me? And a suit?"

"What happened to your gun?" He opened a file folder. "It says you have your own firearm."

"It's, uh, broken and getting fixed. As for the suit, mine has pie all over it. There's a Chinese laundry near the boarding house, but they won't have it clean until tomorrow."

Wentworth pulled a form out of a drawer. "How did you break your gun? Never mind. I don't want to know. Sign on line seven."

19
HALLOWED HALLS OF LEARNING

Miles got off the ferry and wondered why the University of California was on a hillside. He wondered why they didn't build the thing in Sacramento or some other place where the ground was flat. Berkeley had way too many hills.

It took about five minutes before he noticed somebody walking along in one of these ridiculous freshman hats. He decided to follow the young man, lacking any other plan on how to figure out why four men had accosted him and Mabel. The man entered a building that said **Science** on the front door. He quickly descended down a set of stairs that were marked **Basement**. Miles followed as quietly as he could.

At the bottom of the stairs was a door marked **Staff Only**. Another room was marked **Storage**. The storage room was locked. That kind of left the staff room as the best candidate as it was not locked. As he entered, he could hear voices. But he couldn't understand them. Whatever these people were speaking, it certainly was not English.

Miles knew they taught foreign languages in college. And he recognized the language being spoken, even though he'd only heard very little of it once before. He drew his revolver, the one Wentworth had just issued him because Mabel ran off with his. College teaching a course in Martian? That was too hard to accept. He moved into the main room. The man he'd been following was sitting next to some other guy in front of a box that had glowing dials on it. He announced himself, "Federal Agent!" Then someone hit him from behind and he was out cold.

Miles thought there were a few things the Treasury Department needed to put in their job description. Being hit in the head and knocked out seemed like an obvious one. Waking up on the floor of a room seemed like a contender as well. Making that waking up on the floor of a darkened room. He was sure Wentworth would get that taken care of. He sat himself up. Somehow, with no hard evidence, he suspected he was in the room marked **Storage.** Why not have a storage room that had nothing in it—nothing but a Secret Service agent lying on the floor. The university regents must surely have ordered that they leave room for and build a room that shall have nothing in it. Of course they did, because he was sitting in it. Makes perfect sense.

Time was irrelevant with no light and no watch, it could not be measured in any precise sense. Miles was sure he'd been in **Storage** for a lot of it though. He was leaning toward days, not hours.

Finally the lock clicked and the door opened by one of his captors. The familiar shape of a freshman beanie was on his head. "Stinks in here."

You didn't leave me so much as a chamber pot. I couldn't hold it forever. I pooped in the corner and wiped myself off on the wall."

"That is positively disgusting," his captor said.

"Can't hold it forever."

"Here's a poop bucket. When they call for you, use it. Otherwise you'll surely poop your pants." He bent over and placed it on the floor in the middle of the room. Then he turned and walked back for the door.

Miles grabbed the bucket and threw it—striking his captor on the back of the head. Then he picked the bucket up and shoved it over the man's head and knocked him down. Then he kicked the side of the bucket until his captor stopped moving. Miles searched the man's pockets and found a key ring. He also recovered his badge.

After locking his captor inside **Storage** Miles headed over to the area with the mysterious box. His gun was sitting right on top of the device. Strangely, it was no longer loaded. Miles took six more bullets out of his pocket and reloaded the weapon. He thought they were rather sloppy, both in leaving the gun out and not searching him very well when they took him prisoner.

"So there you are," a woman said. "The problem is, these college kids don't know nothin'." It was the waitress who threw the pie on him. "But they've got the parts I need for my project."

"I don't suppose you'd care to tell me what your project

is?" Miles asked.

"Not likely." She moved closer to him. "You are cute. Still, Mabel can have just about anyone she wants. I can't figure out her fascination. Of course, I think mortals are disgusting."

"Tell me something," Miles said. "Why'd you kill the waitress?"

"My change was wrong. She counted out my change and it was wrong, so I killed her."

Miles holstered his revolver. "So, what now?"

"You think I'm going to reveal my plans to some government man?" She pointed at him with a Martian weapon.

"You're very perceptive."

"And you put your gun away. You know who I am."

Miles nodded. "Kevin, I presume."

"I'm impressed Mr. O'Malley. And they say you're a dumb shit. You know that the bullets in your gun won't kill me."

"Alas, I do," Miles agreed.

"Well, tell Mabel to meet me at Golden Gate Park at midnight," Kevin said. "You can come, too. Any police or army, or anybody else and I'll kill them all."

"Uh, it's a big park."

"She can find me. Angels can sense one another."

"I don't understand all this angel and demon stuff. Simply put, why is Mabel after you?"

Kevin let out a short laugh. "Good question. Why isn't Nick after me? Or some demon?" She moved uncomfortably close to Miles. "Believe it or not, Mabel is the toughest angel they've got. I'll bet that surprises you. Nick's nothing. He's all fluff. And the demons, I scare the shit out of them. Good luck figuring this stuff out, Miles. But remember this: For whatever reason, Mabel likes you. That's no small favor."

"Understood, madam."

Kevin grabbed Miles and kissed him. "Still, I don't see it." She walked over to a door labeled **Private**. "I'll be gone when you get your reinforcements here. Do let Hector out of that empty storage room. And don't be too hard on him. He's young and horny. He can't really resist the likes of me." From the other side of the door she added, "And I doubt he understands my evil plan, so what's he going to tell you, anyway?"

20
RIDING AROUND TOWN

"**Now,** the thing is, I have no idea how to find Mabel. She needs to know I found Kevin," Miles told Paul. Paul understood these things. But Paul was a horse and there was not a lot he could do about Miles's dilemma. At least he was back. Hopefully, Mabel brought him back. But Paul didn't talk so who knew how he got back. And still, where was Mabel?

He went to his room. The suit Mabel took and his gun were there on the bed. Not the government issued gun, but his own gun the devil had given him.

"I let that Mabel girl drop off your stuff." Mrs. Wilson was standing in the doorway. "Hope you don't mind."

"Thank you, Mrs. Wilson."

She added, "You're sure gone a lot these days."

"I know. Hopefully, that will change soon."

"Well, you're paying for a lot of meals you're not getting."

"That makes me enjoy the ones I get all the more," Miles said. "Thanks again." He closed the door to his room.

It was nice to be home for supper. It was pot roast—one of Miles's favorites. And it had peas and carrots with it. As he ate his food, his thoughts wandered. It was having meals included that brought him to the rooming house when he arrived in San Francisco. Plus there was space for Paul. All in all, one of the best choices he'd ever made. Having a horse in San Francisco was not simple or cheap. Mrs. Wilson seemed to like Paul for some reason. She never charged anything extra for him to stay there and even fed him if Miles was gone on government business.

"Mrs. Wilson, afraid I'll be out late again tonight."

"What do you do at night?"

"Keeping everyone safe from criminals," Miles said.

"You'd think the criminals would go to bed sometime," she said.

"They never seem to."

After supper, Miles saddled up Paul. At least with a horse, he could cover a lot of ground in and around Golden Gate Park. "Thing is, Paul, I don't know why we're getting involved in this angel stuff. They need to bash each other's brains out in hell or some other place and leave me out of it. Why do I have to go traipsing across creation because the Sioux catch some Martian? I'm tired of this, Paul. I almost wish I was back being a barber."

Miles tied off Paul at the back of the amphitheater. He made his way down to the stage. Everything was so quiet. He wondered why he'd never been there before. Miles had lived in San Francisco for over three years. His vagabond days appeared to be behind him.

As he sat there, he realized the whole thing was bogus. Kevin had lied. He knew where she really was. And he finally figured out what the mysterious device was. "Paul, I'm stupid."

The horse snorted in agreement.

They raced in the direction of Fisherman's Wharf. That was some distance from where they'd been in the park. Miles was glad he had his horse with him. "Whoa!" he pulled back on the reins. There was a woman standing in the street. That wasn't so unusual, but this one was wearing stockings with garter belts and some sort of corset—in public. "Madame Veronica?"

"Hi Miles."

"What's wrong?"

"Could you come back inside? I'm not really dressed."

He was well aware of that. He found a place to tie Paul off and followed her inside. "What's happened?"

"What time is it?"

"Around midnight."

"Oh dear." She sat down. "It's Wentworth."

"What's he done?" Miles asked.

"I fear he's been kidnaped."

"Kidnaped?"

"Around ten o'clock, well everyone else had gone for the day. We don't stay open late—upsets the neighbors even more than our simply being here. Wentworth, he's so sweet…"

"I know he's sweet. Your point?"

"I … we don't … this isn't a brothel."

"I know that. I've been here before. What were you doing

that you don't do?" Miles asked. He was growing impatient. If it had been anyone but Wentworth, he'd have already kissed the matter off.

"I was giving him a hand job."

"Okay. Why were you out in the street?"

"The door burst open. Four men wearing these really stupid blue and gold hats came in. They tied up Wentworth, then hit me in the head with a club of some kind. When I came to, there was nobody else inside the house. The front door was wide open. I went outside and saw you. I had no idea so much time had gone by."

"I think I know who those men are. This may connect to my case I'm working. I've got to go. Try and find a policeman and report this. Tell them you told me and that Wentworth works for the Treasury. You might just say you were, uh, talking and leave that other detail out. I've got to go."

"You can't stay?"

"No. Lives may be at stake. I've got to go."

Miles and Paul raced down to the wharf. The ferries to Oakland did not run at night. Sometimes, fishing boats would straggle in, even after dark. And a few captains even chose to sleep on their boats some of the time. Miles noticed the *Murphy Giant* was just tying off. It appeared to be a steam powered contraption. Smoke was still coming out the exhaust pipe.

"Excuse me, good sir."

"What do you want?" a crusty man with a salt and pepper beard suspiciously asked. "We didn't catch no fish today."

"I'm sorry to hear that, but I do not care. Can you rev back up your engines and take us to Berkeley?"

"Who the hell is *us*?" the fisherman asked.

Miles showed him his badge, "Agent O'Malley, United States Treasury. This is an emergency. The United States government will compensate you for your time."

The fisherman scratched his chin whiskers for a moment. "Well, could use some extra dough with fishing so lousy. But who's *we*?"

"Myself and my horse."

"Why the hell not. Come aboard. I've gotta see how you're getting him to come on this boat."

Miles dismounted and approached the plank. "Paul, I need you in Berkeley. You can do this."

Paul very reluctantly stepped on the plank. His weight caused the boat to rock. Paul jumped and landed on the fishing boat.

"Good boy," Miles said.

21
EVIL PLANS

They were soon underway, heading across San Francisco Bay. "Name's Gus. I better get paid for this."

Miles wrote out a handwritten receipt for one boat charter. "Don't worry, the United States Government pays its bills, or most of them."

"What was that?"

"Nothing, Gus, nothing."

It seemed like an agonizingly long time to get across the bay. In fact, the bay seemed bigger at night for some reason. Finally, they pulled up to the Berkeley pier and they were off. The **Science** building was quiet and locked up.

"You there!" a man was shouting from the darkness. As he approached it was obvious he was wearing a policeman's uniform. "Campus police," he announced. "You can't bring that horse on campus. It's not allowed."

"United States Treasury." Miles displayed his badge. "Special Agent O'Malley. This is serious, Constable. This is really serious. Where would the science students likely live? Most of the ones I'm looking for were freshmen—they had those stupid hats on."

"It's sergeant, actually. Well, if they've joined a frat, it would likely be Epsilon something. Those damned Greek letters, can't remember them all." He pointed north. "Two blocks on your left."

"Thank you, Sergeant," Miles said as he climbed back up on his horse.

"You still can't bring that horse on campus."

"United States government business," Miles declared. He didn't really know what the phrase meant, but no one else did, either. He raced his horse down the street.

Miles found the frat house. He was surprised that torch lights had been set up in the back yard.

Kevin raised her glass. "To Wentworth."

"To Wentworth," the twenty students repeated. Everyone took a sip of wine.

"Dig in everyone." She took the warming covers off the plates to reveal various cuts of cooked meat with some type of gravy on them. One plate remained covered. "Seems we have one more for supper. Agent Miles O'Malley, everyone. Agent O'Malley, Wentworth is already representing the Secret Service, but please join us."

Miles approached the table. They were in the back yard of the fraternity. Wooden picnic tables had been set up. "Okay, where is Wentworth then?"

"Why, right here," Kevin said. She lifted the final cover off the last platter. It revealed Wentworth's head. "Dig in. He's absolutely delicious."

A couple of the freshmen threw up.

"Boys, where is your sense of adventure?" She looked at some of the puke pouring out of one student. "Hopeless. I buy them liquor. I even got them all prostitutes last night. God knows I'm not going to fuck them. And this is the thanks I get— puking all over my special party. Agent O'Malley is not puking. He's a man—not some boy like you lot. Oh well, the prostitutes were just an act of kindness. I didn't think any of you should die virgins. I suspect they were all virgins, frankly. Although Larry, the blond boy on the end, well his prostitute said he had a very large thing and it gave her immense pleasure. Yet he's so shy."

She took another sip of wine. "I thought that was real nice of me." She looked over Miles. "He's not a virgin—oh no. He's been banging my sister for quite some time. But no matter." She whistled. The back door to the fraternity opened and twenty-five little green men in silver colored suits poured out of the building. Some of them had the beam weapons like the ones in the Black Hills. They each carried large, serrated knives, which were housed on holsters on their belts. The screaming stopped after about a minute. "Cooked or raw, eat your pleasure."

Kevin smiled at Miles. "Mars is a dying planet. But they don't really want to live here. That got me thinking. They don't like Earth's gravity or its high oxygen content. But they could harvest its water, its food, its animals and keep things going on

Mars for a very long time. So, here they are. My secret plan. And they don't even know it themselves. They think I'm a man for some reason." She took a bite out of Wentworth's head. "My secret plan. What do you think, Agent O'Malley? Wentworth is absolutely delicious. Please try some. As you can see, Group Commander War likes him just fine. Want some more, Group Commander?"

She took a sip of wine. "You screw my beautiful sister. But do you know her? Any idea why she's here to stop me?"

Miles noticed Mabel was in the shadows. She untied Paul, then whispered something in his ear. The horse ran off.

"You'd think Nick—or we remember when he went by Lucifer—you might think he'd man up and deal with me. But no. And the demons—they're all scared of me. For good reason, I might add. I write demon recipes on the wall of my room. Yum. Actually, demons taste like shit. Not like Wentworth here. So moist and juicy.

"And that God. He sent just two cherubs to get the job done. Well, they weren't nearly enough. Boy, I'll tell you, cherubs really taste like shit. You wouldn't want to eat them."

Kevin belched, loudly. "So, God goes and gets my little sister to come and destroy me. Why sis? You and Miles could be screwing right now." She patted the wooden table. "We could make it a threesome. But no, she plots to destroy me. That's no fun."

"It is God's will," Mabel said.

"Honey, He kicked you out of Heaven. You don't owe Him anything."

"It is still God's will, nonetheless, and I will stop you," Mabel warned.

Now that she was in the light, Miles noticed Mabel was wearing a white robe of some kind. She had a golden helmet on. And she was carrying something that looked like a small sword, also with a golden color to it. She was hardly dressed like the Mabel he was used to.

"They are eating Wentworth," Miles said.

"Kind of my way of poking my thumb in the eye of the United States government," Kevin said. "You really should try some. He was very good."

Mabel went over to one of the little green men and asked him something in Martian. She looked back at Miles. "These are the same guys from the Black Hills, Miles."

"Really?"

"The exact same ones," Mabel repeated

"You are a few bricks short, aren't you, Miles." Kevin said. "She's trying to tell you these are the same Martians you encountered with the now late General Grant." She stared at Miles for a moment. "She thinks this is all they've got. There is no big fleet of Martians—this is it. Don't you see it, Miles? She thinks I didn't check things out. That I didn't go over to the observatory and look at Mars. I know there are few of them left. I don't care, dear sister. As long as they wipe out humanity—nothing else matters. Now go back to hell before you get yourself hurt."

One of the Martians fired his beam weapon at Mabel. She deflected it with her sword. Then she drew a revolver and fired six rounds into the Martians. Mabel took away a beam weapon from one of the remaining Martians and started shooting. In seconds, the Martians all laid dead on the ground.

Clap-clap-clap. "You've saved the world. Big deal," Kevin said.

"Hands in the air! Oh my god." The sergeant didn't seem to know who to point his firearm at.

"Sergeant, you are in incredible danger. Get out of here," Miles warned.

Kevin grabbed Mabel's sword out of her hand and threw it like a spear. It went right through the campus police sergeant.

"Sister, sister don't got no more bullets to play with," Kevin taunted. "Sister, sister, don't got the Sword of Damocles no more." Kevin moved over to Mabel and grabbed her and kissed her on the mouth. "What's next angel pooh? Behold, the good little angel from hell is out of tricks. And I am going to turn this whole world into one giant hell. And Nick and God can try and stop me—if they have the balls. That's so funny, the thought of Nick and God working together. My guess is one will cower in heaven and the other in hell and that will be that." Kevin took another sip of wine. "You really should have some Wentworth. It's really good." She came over to Miles. "And this man, this pitiful secret agent..."

"Special Agent."

"You are special. You got to screw my sister. At least Miles had the balls to try and stop me. Nick Mephistopheles sure didn't. Oh, keep her confined in hell. You know how easy it was to bribe a demon to let me out, Miles? Of course you don't. And now what happens? Sister, you can join me. We don't have to fight."

"It is God's will. I will fight with every breath I have," Mabel said.

"How about you, then, Special Secret Agent Miles O'Malley? Where'd your horse go?"

"He doesn't like violence."

"Want to join me? I'll let you have your way with me." She pulled the sword out of the wall. The policeman's body slid to the ground. "Do you know why this sword is special, Miles?"

Miles replied, "It is made out of titanium, the metal used to kill the Titans, or so they say. It is believed to be capable of killing an angel as well."

"I'm surprised you knew that. Nick didn't think you were very bright," Kevin said. She went back over to the table area and picked up the empty revolver. "The Devil's Gun! The gun that never misses. My sister brought it to kill me tonight, and shot up the remaining bullets, the last six remaining bullets made out of titanium. The last six shot Martians who would have happily died from lead bullets. Sister made a boo-boo. Sister, don't make me force you to suffer. Bend over and let me lob your head off and be done with this."

Mabel knelt before her sister. "It is God's will."

"So she keeps saying. Now, Miles, this won't be easy to watch. But I'll kill you after I do her."

"No, I don't think so," Miles said. The report of a gunshot rang out. Then a second. Then a third.

Kevin bent over and clutched the three holes in her chest. "What?"

"The devil's gun never misses." He held his gun up in the light. "Nick gave me one of them. There actually are two of them. They're a set." He fired another round into her. "And, well, I lied about the last six bullets. There were a few more

I'd hidden away. You only thought the ones Mabel shot were the last ones." He fired another round. This bullet struck her between the eyes. Her body dropped to the ground like a bag of potatoes.

There was someone else in the shadows—on horseback.

"Get off my horse," Miles demanded.

He dismounted. "Now Miles, Paul came and got me. And here I am."

"It's safe now," Mabel said with her voice quivering in anger. "She's dead."

"So I can see," Nick said. "Alas, so are all these frat boys. And the Martians. And this dead, cooked fellow. What a disgusting display."

"I didn't let her out. Once again, I had to clean up your mess for you," Mabel snapped.

"This isn't very clean, my dear."

"I..." She couldn't figure out what to say.

"Besides, it was Miles who saved the day. I've been uneasy with those titanium bullets being out in the world. They are one of the very few things that can kill an angel."

"Even you," Miles pointed out.

"Even me," he agreed.

"So, now what?" Mabel asked.

"Some, er, special people will be here in a few minutes. The Martian bodies and the frat boys will never be seen again. Miles, go home as soon as the morning ferries start running. And Mabel, I think hell is the place for you."

As Miles started to get up on his horse, Nick grabbed his shoulder. "Make this a lesson, Miles. You messed with things you don't understand. You got lucky. She planned to kill millions. And poor Wentworth sure didn't need this."

Miles was surprised. "You knew Wentworth?"

"We both liked to visit a certain establishment here in town."

"Madame Veronica is a model of discretion," Miles said. "Remember this, Nick. I had no real quarrel with you before now. But I blame you for what happened to Wentworth. Kevin was one of your people. And this mess was your goddamned fault—not mine. So go back to hell where you belong. And stay there."

Miles looked at Mabel, but he was at a loss for words of what to say to her. "Come on, Paul. Let's go."

Nick watched him ride off. "He's not the shy, good-hearted kid we once knew, is he?"

"No," Mabel said. "That's why I like him."

"You are hopeless. Now give me back my gun and let's get out of here."

The crew all wore white uniforms. The bleach they poured out destroyed the blood—especially the green Martian blood. They stopped for a break and decided what was left of Wentworth was very good.

22
STRATEGIC POSITIONS

It was around 10 a.m. when Miles finally made it back to the United States Courthouse in San Francisco. The first ferry from Berkeley had broken down. Ferries were more frequent from Oakland. Persistent waiting eventually got Miles and his horse across the bay. In the interim, he'd sent a telegram that Wentworth was dead. He was not sure if any of the other agents were in town to read it. And he had absolutely no idea if the San Francisco Police had acted on Madame Veronica's report about Wentworth's kidnaping. Questions seemed to be about all Miles had.

The stairs up to the third floor seemed especially tiring. The door was unlocked. He opened it, not quite knowing who might be inside or what that individual might know.

Major Yeats was sitting at a chair. A man Miles did not recognize was reading something off a clipboard. Where Major Yeats was a tall man with red hair and a matching moustache, this other fellow seemed small in stature—and bald.

"Agent O'Malley this is Assistant Director Curtis Melbourne," Yeats introduced.

"'Change locks on doors. Wentworth dead. Will explain when return.' Your telegram seems a bit scant in detail, Agent O'Malley."

"I can't put stuff like this on an unsecured telegram." He handed a report he'd scribbled out on the ferry. "I got back as fast as I could." Miles plopped down in the other vacant chair. "Dang I'm tired."

"The new keys are being made as we speak," Melbourne said. "I am somewhat concerned one of our people was last seen at a place like Madame Veronica's."

"Sir, how did you get here so fast?" Miles asked. "I only wired in a few hours ago."

"Your wire did not bring me here or Major Yeats for that matter," the assistant director explained. "We were coming here anyway. As I read your report, I am glad we did."

"Why is that?" Miles asked. His report left out certain things, such as Mabel and Nick—but it did include the freshmen and the Martians and a mysterious woman leading them named Kevin, whereabouts unknown.

"Them Martians," the major said. "They're camped in the Oakland hills. The army is ferrying two thousand men from the Presidio in about an hour."

"Oh, hell," Miles said. "I'm so tired."

"Tired is what we do, Agent O'Malley," the assistant director said. "We've got a ferry to catch."

As they walked down the stairs, Miles asked Yeats, "Who's minding the store?"

"We have not got anyone. The door is locked."

"I could've stayed over in Berkeley," Miles said.

Paul didn't like the swaying of the boat. The Navy's ferry, which normally took men back and forth to Oakland from Treasure Island in the middle of the bay, was grossly overloaded. Miles was convinced it would capsize at any moment and the soldiers, artillery pieces and his horse would all go to the bottom of the bay and die. The choppy waves reinforced that theory.

Melbourne seemed a bit green in color. Just a little more and he might even pass for a Martian. The boat came into the Oakland pier and the troops and equipment quickly disembarked. Miles climbed up on his horse. He noted the major had his horse with him. There was a driver and a buggy waiting for Melbourne.

"Why is this a Secret Service matter?" Miles asked the major when they were out of earshot of their assistant director.

"Beats me. You know how Washington gets—everyone is always fighting for their piece of turf."

"Let the War Department have it," Miles said. "This will end very badly."

"How so?"

Miles shook his head. "These Martians, they are bad news."

Sulphur was one mineral Mabel wondered why they made it. It apparently had some medicinal value, for what exactly, she did not know. But so much of hell stunk of the stuff as it boiled up from the big lake. Her thoughts returned to her current predicament. "Well how come you gave Miles one and you won't give me one?"

"Miles uses his responsibly. You gamble yours away—constantly. And you don't need one." Nick leaned back in his chair. "I am tired of this conversation. You will stay in your room and that's that."

"I had a gun when the Martians came."

"And you wasted some very precious titanium bullets on them instead of your horrible sister."

"It all worked out."

"Because Miles had the second gun and the rest of the special bullets. And you put him in the position of killing an angel. I have no idea what the ramifications of that are going to be."

"But…"

"Mabel," Nick pointed at his door, "be gone."

"But my clothes are still in San Francisco," she protested. "At the Chinese laundry."

"I do not care. We have plenty of those angel robes. Frankly, I do not care if you go naked. This conversation is over."

"Well, you're a pooh head." Mabel stormed out of Nick's office. She noticed Ellul was following her. "Are you following me?"

"Mister said to lock you in your room."

She stopped and slipped out of her robe. "I've had it with this robe." She went inside her room and slammed the door.

A few seconds later she could hear the door being locked. She checked the door. It was locked. How long this time? She figured it wouldn't be more than a century. She could do that without even trying. But Miles would be dead by the time she got out. And her clothes. She spent a lot of counterfeit money in New York having those clothes made. Now some skinny women at some laundry were going to end up with them. This was horrible.

As she looked out the window she said, "Thanks God. Last time I do you a favor." She decided to comb her hair, although there wasn't anyone to impress. Maybe she could be like that girl in the fairy tale—the slutty one, Rapunzel, who had lovers climb up her hair and into the tower. Who would be there to climb up? Hell was full of scumbags and lawyers and lawyer scumbags. And demons were disgusting. It was no wonder she was always leaving hell to go have fun. Nick was such a pooh head. There wasn't any fun in hell.

Maybe she could get some whips and chains and save Nick the trouble of going all the way to San Francisco to see Mistress Veronica. Or was it Madame Veronica? Scratch that thought. That was weird, even for her. Although whipping Nick did seem like fun somehow.

She wondered what the Martians were up to. They were even worse than demons. And they smelled like mildew. Why would Kevin team up with the likes of them? At least she didn't screw the freshmen. At least Kevin had some standards. She missed her sister. Sure she was wicked and a cannibal, but they were sisters.

She caught herself rubbing her necklace. Just to know, she tried the platinum key on her door. It unlocked. Interesting. She put one of those baggy robes on. Running around naked might bring too much attention, if not in hell, certainly in San Francisco.

"What do you want me to do?" Ellul asked his lord and master.
    "Do?"
    "Angel Mabel is gone again."
    "What's your point?" Nick asked.
    "She is gone," the demon told his master.
    "So it would seem."
    "Do you want me to track her down?"
    "No. She's simply being Mabel. Let her be," Nick said.

The teller eyed her suspiciously. He wondered if she was one of those homeless people he'd heard about. She certainly was not dressed like the other customers in the Mercantile Bank of San Francisco. "May I help you?" She smiled. She was very pretty for a homeless person. He wondered how many illegitimate children she had. Breeding children and begging for money was what these people did.

"I need into my safe deposit box. It's number 234."

"One moment." He put a closed sign in his teller cage window. "I'll meet you at the end of the counter." He looked up the signature card for that box and handed her a form to sign. She signed it and handed it back. The signature matched, to his surprise. "Right this way." He put the bank's key in one of the locks and took her key and inserted it into the other one. It matched as well. The little rectangular door opened. He pulled the box out and took it over to one of the customer booths. "Let me know when you're finished."

Mabel opened the box. She was down to her last hundred thousand in counterfeit money. She was going to have to economize. No more living in hotels. She thought about the rooming house Miles lived at, but that might be too plain. Then she thought of a place to live that would be just about perfect. She put twenty thousand dollars in a paper bag and summoned the teller to return the box.

The cable car swiftly carried her across town. She knocked on the door. After quite some time, it opened. A short woman dressed in leather was standing there. "The maid position has been filled." She started to close the door.

"I'm here to see Madame Veronica."

"That's what they all say."

The thought of being mistaken for a maid. Then, she remembered she was still wearing the baggy angel robe. No wonder the cable car conductor tried to leave the Montgomery Street start of the line early when he saw her coming.

Madame Veronica eventually made it to the door. "Yes?"

"It's me, Mabel."

"I don't know anyone named Mabel." She slammed the door shut.

That did not work out quite the way she'd imagined.

"Hey toots, that's a high class place over there. Come down to the wharf and stay with us." She wasn't sure which loudmouth it was who said it. There were four men to choose from—all dressed as fishermen. She was starting to wish she'd stayed in hell. It was getting late and all the businesses were closing.

She decided to try Miles and made her way across town

to his rooming house. Naturally, he was not there. She went around back and thought she'd ask Paul where Miles was. The little barn was empty. Paul was not there, either. She piled some hay in the corner and decided to sleep until morning when, hopefully, she could get her clothes from the laundry. If this was what poor people lived like, she wanted no part of it.

Finally, mercifully, the sun came back up and the city came back to life. The Wing Chinese Laundry opened at seven o'clock. She was first in line. Her clothes were nice and clean. If only she had somewhere to put them.

Two men in business suits were waiting for her when she came back out of the laundry. "You men aren't from the Treasury Department, are you?"

"No, ma'am, we are not," they insisted.

"Do you gentlemen, by chance, have change for a hundred? The way I'm dressed, no one would take my money," Mabel said. "I slept in somebody's back yard last night."

23
LET THERE BE WAR

It was nice that the army provided a pup tent. The assistant director and Major Yeats, now in uniform although he was supposedly retired from the army, were in a tent right next to his. Paul was off in a makeshift corral getting pampered by some horse attendant called Festus.

Miles wondered how come these things always happened on land. The navy had much better food. The army beans were tough and chewy, The biscuits tasted like the ones he made. That's what's for supper in an army camp. Even the coffee left a lot to be desired. And the apricot cobbler—that brought back some memories.

The navy knew how to make beans. His official duties once carried him all the way to Los Angeles, in southern California, on a navy ship. And their beans were always perfectly seasoned and tender. Inside the confines of a ship, well beans are prone to certain developments. Those developments, in a confined space, could be problematic. On the other hand, farting in a pup tent didn't seem that much different. But Miles was much more partial to navy chow. He'd rather have Mrs. Wilson's pork chops. But that was not likely unless Mrs. Wilson joined the army and was assigned to the local catering corps.

"General Grant spoke quite highly of you," the assistant director said. "Said you could be counted on when the going gets rough."

"The general was a good man," Miles muffled out of his mouth. The army biscuits were so dry it was a challenge to get them down.

"That's interesting," Major Yeats said. A new wagon had just arrived. There was a driver and someone in back, in an army uniform.

"Supposed to be a Martian interpreter," the assistant director said. "Mind me, I don't see how anyone could learn Martian. What? He'd go to Mars on a balloon ride? But that's what they say, anyhow."

Miles and Major Yeats spent the night sleeping on the ground in a pup tent provided by the army. It made Miles really miss his warm bed back at Mrs. Wilson's. At daybreak there was some guy bugling Reveille. Miles staggered out of the tent. He found the chow line and got some eggs and biscuits.

Miles found his horse was chomping away on a large pile of food. "This your horse, mister?"

"He is. I'm Miles O'Malley, with the U. S. Treasury."

"Treasury has their own horses?"

"A few."

"Name's Festus. Been looking after horses pert near thirty year now. This one, well I noticed he didn't have an army brand on him. Well, he's a right fine horse."

As they rode up into the Oakland Hills, Miles asked, "What is it we're doing here again?"

"We're watching the army get slaughtered with beam weapons. You started this, O'Malley," the assistant director said.

"I started it? How the heck did I start it?" Miles asked.

"Back in the Black Hills. Your orders were to kill the Martians, not let them go."

"My orders were to do whatever General Grant wanted. And he said to let them go. There was no way to win the fight."

The three Treasury "observers" were put in line behind a column of infantry. They started up a trail into the Oakland Hills. No one had told them exactly where they were going. This was a fairly large area that went from Tilden Meadows above Berkeley all the way down to a range of hills above San Leandro. Miles hoped whoever was at the front of the line knew where they were headed.

A couple of officers raced by the column of infantry. Someone said the "Martian Interpreter" was with them. Miles couldn't get a good look at him as they raced by so fast and were so far away.

"Well, at least they can mow down all the soldiers and give us time to get away," Miles said.

"He always this gloomy?" Melbourne asked.

"Yep," Major Yeats agreed.

"You don't talk much, do you, Yeats?"

"Nope."

As they advanced into the hills, they approached Tilden Meadow. There sat ten Martian spheres and about fifty green guys in silver suits were dug in along a ridge line. The army interpreter and two officers were approaching the Martians with a white flag.

Paul seemed to be getting increasingly agitated. Miles asked him, "Are they going to attack?" At about that moment his brain caught up with things. He knew who the interpreter was and Paul did, too.

An officer rode up to the three of them. "I'm Lt. Colonel Crabtree. Which one of you is O'Malley?"

"Me," Miles answered,

"You dealt with the Martians in the Dakotas?"

"Yes."

"Their strategy makes no sense. If they can fly and we sure as hell can't, why risk our artillery, which is setting up as we speak?"

"Because they don't fear your men and don't think your weapons can harm them. They prove that and humans will cave into their demands."

"It's a risky strategy."

"Colonel, Mars is a dying world. I don't think they have a lot more of these spheres and men than what you see here. If we can't reason with them—annihilate them."

"Come with me to see General Calhoun," he said.

Miles followed along as they raced up the hill and past the infantry column. Yep, as he got closer he certainly knew the interpreter. It was clearly Mabel. They had her dressed as a man, since that had been a problem before—but that was no man.

There was Mabel next to some guy holding a large white flag talking to some green guy in a silver suit. The interpreter came back to Col. Crabtree. She briefly smiled at Miles. "Sir, they basically said Earth will surrender twenty percent of its food and agriculture, plus one million people to be used as slaves."

"Or?"

"Or they will exterminate all life on Earth and find what they want someplace else."

"Signal, attack signal, open fire," the colonel ordered.

A heliograph flashed a signal to the artillery battery. They immediately started attacking the Martian position. As the firing got underway, two of the spheres rose off the ground and floated away from the battle action.

"This is going to end badly," Major Yeats said.

"That sounds like something I'd say," Miles offered. "And I think you're right."

Blue light rays started firing back from the Martian positions. In less than a minute the artillery battery was silent. Then the rays turned on the advancing infantry. The two spheres that had taken off returned and were hovering overhead.

"Those spheres, they're directing the Martian fire just like we do with a forward observer—which we are lacking in this campaign," the major pointed out.

"Fat lot of good that does us," the assistant director said.

Colonel Crabtree rode up on his horse. He was with a pack horse that seemed pretty loaded down. "Gentlemen, as we discussed." And he rode off toward the artillery battery. Paul and Miles were hoping to head off in the other direction. But the major and Assistant Director Melbourne obediently followed after the colonel. Miles followed along as well.

The colonel grabbed the first cannon they came to and swabbed it out with water. "What we're about to see is a top secret weapon that does not exist."

"Understood," the major agreed.

"The Grasshopper Project is a way to get more out of our artillery." He stuffed a bag of powder and took a strange looking artillery shell that seemed to have wings. The major prepared the torch and inserted a fuse. It looked elongated and bug-like—and green.

"Fire!" the colonel ordered.

The cannon roared and a strange object that looked like an insect flew out of the cannon. Two seconds later, it attached to one of the Martian ships. Two more seconds and there was a powerful explosion. The Martian ship began to spin violently, then crashed to the ground. Smoke began to pour out of a crack in the crashed sphere.

"We're awfully vulnerable standing out here in the open," Miles pointed out.

"Fire!" the colonel ordered.

Another of the strange artillery shells flew out and attached itself. In seconds, the second hovering craft dropped to earth.

"Earth's gravity is a lot stronger than Mars," the colonel explained. "It doesn't take a lot to bring one of these down."

The eight remaining spheres took off into the air. "Fire!" the colonel yelled.

The major ignited the cannon and another grasshopper shell launched. It embedded in a sphere and exploded, sending that ship back to earth. The rest of the ships hightailed it into the air and were soon gone from sight.

The green guys fought to the death. Not a single one of them surrendered even though their buddies flew off and abandoned them. Their bodies were dumped in mass graves and the camp was broken down and hauled away by sundown. The navy could sail at night and the ferry taking the troops back to the Presidio soon docked in the city.

24
CONSULTANT

Miles and Paul headed for home. Miles wanted to sleep in his own bed and Paul was quite ready to get away from sailing around in boats.

After putting his horse away, Miles ventured inside and relaxed in the parlor for a bit. He was pleased to find the evening edition of *The Examiner* was still around. It was fascinating that the army held war games for training new troops in the Oakland Hills and they had been a splendid success.

The next morning he headed for the United States Courthouse. He found the assistant director there and someone he did not know. "Miles O'Malley, this is Wentworth."

"No he isn't."

"Yes he is."

"Yes I am," Wentworth said. "Seriously, my given name is Charles J. Wentworth III. The Wentworth you knew was my cousin."

"Oh." Miles suddenly felt stupid—even for Miles.

"He'll be running the office for the time being," the assistant director said. "Major Yeats will be on assignment for a few days. "That means you are, once again, the only available agent west of Denver. Try not to screw anything up."

"I'll do my best, sir."

"I know things have not been easy for you. We catch any strange or unorthodox case that comes up. Except for U.S. Marshals, the Treasury is the only federal law enforcement agency. And we never use U.S. Marshals because..."

"They're a bunch of drunks," Miles and Yeats both said.

"Good day, gentlemen." The assistant director put a hat on top of his bald head and left.

Wentworth handed him a note. It directed him to go to the War Department Office of Intelligence at the Presidio, room 123, basement.

Miles found it interesting in that he knew nothing of an

Office of Intelligence at the Presidio and couldn't possibly understand why they would want him. "Official business?"

"Sure looks like it," Wentworth said.

"Then I'll take a horse-drawn cab and bring you a receipt."

Wentworth immediately countered with, "How about you'll take a cable car and walk the remaining five blocks? The same reason you're our only agent is the same reason I have to watch your expenses. Congress has not been in a generous mood."

"Very well," Miles agreed. This Wentworth was going to be about like the last one, he feared. "Oh." He plopped down the revolver he temporarily used before his devil's gun came back. "I'm through with this. My own gun has been repaired."

"Very well, Agent O'Malley. Uh, one last thing. My cousin … apparently he was rather fond of some place in his appointment diary. I've never heard of it." He opened up a well worn leather book. "Know anything about a Madame Veronica over on Sansome?"

"Uh, I think they give massages and neck rubs. He was under a lot of stress. Too many cases and not nearly enough funding. A good massage can take that stress right out of you."

"Ah, I see."

It had been a bold face lie. Miles couldn't wait to see how the new Wentworth was going to handle a dominatrix. "I'll be going, then."

He wondered where Wentworth came from. There were few federal employees of any stripe in San Francisco—let alone a fully trained Treasury Department bureaucrat. He reasoned some things were above his pay grade.

Why did the War Department want him? Miles kept wondering. He didn't have any particular knowledge about military matters. He didn't even want to go on the recent Oakland campaign but the assistant director made him.

But there was the prescribed office. He turned the knob and opened the door. A man in a suit sat behind a desk. "Ah, Agent O'Malley, do come in."

That was weird enough, then he added, "I'll tell the director you're here. Do have a seat."

Miles sat on a chair near the door and wondered why he was at this particular place. After a few minutes Col. Crabtree emerged. He was not in uniform, but wore a tan business suit. "Nice to see you again, Agent O'Malley. Right this way." The colonel took him to an office that had a view of the Pacific Ocean, or more accurately the Golden Gate Straight. "You are probably wondering why I sent for you."

"You could say that," Miles agreed.

"Well, we appreciated your help on our recent campaign. Major Yeats has been consulting with us for some time on the grasshopper artillery project. The concept was designed, I am sad to say, to exterminate Indian tribes. We're not proud of that chapter in the army but recognize our country and even the entire world face threats and we need more and better weapons to face them."

"That makes sense," Miles agreed.

"We were very pleased with what was a prototype weapon and we learned a lot. We're developing better aiming abilities and such—we didn't expect we'd be shooting at airborne objects and that's going to require training and such. But, obviously, that has nothing to do with the Secret Service."

There was a knock at the door. "Enter," the colonel said.

The door opened. "Hi Miles." It was Mabel and she no longer was dressed to look like a man.

"Uh."

"I got a job Miles. I'm teaching the Martian language to some of the intelligence officers. And I'm consulting on a few things."

"She is quite modest. She has saved us thousands of man hours on this Martian situation," the colonel offered. "I asked Miss Saunders why she thinks the Martians were dealing with this Kevin, who clearly did not look like a man. I wanted your take on her theory as you two are the only surviving attendees of their little party."

That made Miles a bit uneasy. He didn't recall telling anyone Mabel had been there.

"Well, I don't know what the Martians know or don't know about us, but Kevin is generally regarded as a boy's name. Their wireless dealings were with a Kevin they had not seen. When they came out of the frat house they may have thought the actual Kevin was a cook, as she had cooked Wentworth as we understand it. They may have been expecting someone else, a someone who only existed in their own imaginations."

"Agent O'Malley, it seems reasonable. When the shooting started, things went crazy. The frat boys are all dead. We may never know the whole story."

Miles was waiting for someone to mention the lack of Mabel in his report—or how they found Mabel to recruit her. No one did.

"Thank you for coming, Agent O'Malley." The colonel went over and opened the door.

Miles was escorted out of the building by a soldier and he soon found himself walking back to the cable car drop off.

It was pork chop night. That was Miles's favorite. He'd missed the last two on business. It was nice to be home and able to relax a bit. After supper he went out to check on Paul. He wasn't entirely surprised to see Mabel there.

"Hi Miles."

"How did Col. Crabtree know you were there at the college? It wasn't in my report." Miles asked.

"They've had me under surveillance for months."

"Why didn't you mention this?"

She shrugged. "I thought they were Pinkertons, actually. I was wrong."

That did not add up to Miles's thinking. "Who would hire Pinkertons to watch you?"

"Nick."

"Oh."

"Are you okay?" Mabel asked.

"Sure, why wouldn't I be?"

"You had to kill Kevin. It's upsetting when decent people take a life, even by accident," Mabel said. "So I was worried about you."

"That's the thing, I don't feel anything. I don't know if it was because, as you say, she was not a flimsy mortal girl, or she was just plain crazy. I just don't feel anything and I suppose that is not normal or good."

"Twas God's will, if that helps."

"Not really." Miles thought for a moment. "God's will? Really?"

"God told me I had to stop Kevin by any means necessary."

"And you're still. Uh, friendly with God."

"He is still God. I did what God directed. Don't try to figure it out and it'll be better."

"Where are you living?" Miles asked. "You're not in the Claremont anymore?"

"Oh, I rented a room from Madame Veronica."

"Maybe she'll teach you her trade secrets."

"That might be fun," Mabel said.

"Not changing the subject, these guys just showed up and said they wanted to talk to me. Then they showed me badges," Mabel said.

"The War Department has people with badges? That's news."

"And they took me to the Presidio and introduced me to Col. Crabtree. I asked if this was about those horrible freshmen. And then they were offering me a job. Boy, Nick's head will explode." She smiled at the thought of that.

Miles tried to envision such an occurrence. "Yeah, he might."

"Then Madame Veronica offered me a room and I'm an upstanding citizen, just like that."

"Do they, the War Department, not Madame Veronica, know what you are?" Miles asked.

"I'm not sure. They certainly know I'm not your ordinary girl. But, whether they think I'm an angel—I'm just not sure. Let's go inside."

"Okay."

"It's Muffin, right?" Mrs. Wilson asked.

"Mabel," Miles corrected.

"So she is." Mrs. Wilson reluctantly got out of the way for Miles and Mabel to go into the parlor.

"Next time you'll have to come see me at Madame Veronica's," Mabel loudly teased.

"There's nothing wrong with her hearing," Miles whispered.

"Didn't want her to miss anything. Some shameless hussy coming by a man's home and by herself no less. What is this world coming to?"

25
MEN IN SUITS

"**Miss Saunders?**" Col. Crabtree asked. "Could you step into my office?"

"What can I do for you, sir?"

"Are you and Agent O'Malley romantically involved?"

"Yes."

"Normally I would consider it inappropriate to ask. We are dealing with classified and secret information here."

"I'm not sure I understand. Agent O'Malley doesn't talk to me about his cases. Frankly, I don't talk about mine because I'm new at this."

"Well, we at the War Department don't really like letting Treasury in our business. The thing is, our agents don't really have any arrest power. The Treasury Department and the U.S. Marshals are the only agencies that have federal arrest powers. We don't like to use the marshals as they're a bunch of drunks. That means if I want to legally have somebody arrested I have to go to your friend or Major Yeats. And Yeats has spent half his time helping us develop new weapons. He was an artillery instructor at West Point before retiring from the army and joining the Secret Service."

"I'm not sure what that has to do with me?"

"I need someone arrested, but I don't want it known that we're behind it. Can you get O'Malley to do it?"

"I can try," Mabel agreed.

"Splendid," the colonel replied as he handed her a large file envelope.

"But you are wrong," Mabel said. "Wentworth could affect an arrest."

"Wentworth? He's a pencil pusher?"

"Case Supervisor IV of the United States Treasury. Look it up."

"How do you know these things?" Crabtree asked.

"When the other Wentworth was eaten at the cannibal

party I wanted to apply, but I can't because I'm a woman."

"Oh."

"Blasted Congress," Wentworth called out from behind a file folder. "Every blasted time we get Martians or ghosts or zombies we have to send an agent to deal with it, yet Congress keeps cutting our budget."

"Zombies?"

"Oh, that was one of Yeats's cases. Point is, we just don't have the manpower to handle everything they keep dumping on us. Now they want me to drop everything and run over to the Presidio. I have half a mind to simply not show up."

"You'll go, Wentworth," Miles said. "Besides, I came across this right before your cousin got eaten by those horrible college students."

"Inter Agency Expense Voucher." Wentworth read on with the filing and documentation instructions. "Fascinating. So, we can bill the army for my having to run over there at their back and call."

"We sure can."

"They've got plenty of money in their budget. What's one less Gatling gun, right?" Wentworth was smiling. He never smiled. "I can bill them and we get more money out of their budget. If only I knew their budget codes."

"War Department, Office of Intelligence, Presidio is 84-39-457P," Miles said.

"How did you discover that?"

"It's right here in this book: *Everything You Need to Know about Your United States Government*. It's amazing," Miles said. "When Paul needed oats when I went to Reno to pick up the fake silver bars, the other Wentworth billed the Federal Reserve Bank for them."

"Fake silver bars?"

"Oh, Judge Hastings was furious. But the point was we kissed the expense off to somebody else. Your cousin was a genius at that," Miles said. "This is my copy. You can borrow it, but I want it back. You can bill your own copy to the Agriculture Department."

"Why would we bill the Agriculture Department?"

Wentworth asked.

"We haven't stuck them with anything yet."

"Fascinating."

The door knocked for the second time. Where was that colored lady? Blanche? "Oh Blanche, there's someone. Never mind. I'll get it myself." Mabel opened the front door. "Why hello, Wentworth. Do come in."

"Uh, perhaps I'm at the wrong address," he said.

"Nonsense. Come right on it."

"What are you doing here, Miss Saunders?" he asked.

"I live here. I rent a room."

"Oh."

'Well right this way."

Wentworth said, "I was told I could get a massage here."

"Of course," Mabel agreed. "Wait here. Someone will be along shortly."

"Did someone come in?" Blanche asked.

"Yes. I put him in the first room." Mabel tried to suppress her giggling.

"Did he say what he wanted?" Blanche asked.

"Something about getting tied up," Mabel said.

"I'll tell Madame Veronica."

"You do that," Mabel said between giggles. "Wentworth is in for quite an evening."

"What are you giggling about, Miss Mabel?"

"I don't know. It just came over me."

An hour later, Mabel heard the door open and Madame Veronica said. "I'm so sorry, Mr. Wentworth." Then the door closed. "What does he think we are, a massage parlor? After an hour, mind you."

"Did you charge him?" Blanche asked.

"You're dang right I did. I wouldn't unlock him until he paid up."

Miles thought the new Wentworth looked rather tired. "Everything okay, Wentworth?"

"Shouldn't it ought to be?"

"What?"

"Oh, that place you thought gives massages, well they don't." He seemed a bit cross.

"Sorry to hear that, Wentworth," Miles said. He was struggling really hard to keep from giggling.

Some soldier came in and handed Wentworth a large envelope. "Ah, it appears in good order," said Wentworth. He noted something down in a ledger. "Major Yeats."

The major emerged from the file room. "What?"

"I need you and Agent O'Malley to perform an arrest."

"Where at?" the major asked.

"The University of California."

"Oh, I hate Berkeley," Miles complained. "Who are we arresting?"

"The warrant is for Ezra B. Cunningham, PhD."

"Shouldn't be too hard to find him," the major said. "What's the charge?"

"Misappropriating federal funds. It says he took grant money to look for oil and used it to build a wireless device to communicate with unnamed extraterrestrials."

"Unnamed my ass," the major said.

"Good day, gentlemen," Wentworth said.

"This sounds completely bogus," Miles said. "Let's go fishing."

"What about the warrant?" the major asked.

"Who wants to go to Berkeley?" The Treasury Department was housed on the third floor of the courthouse. The U.S. Marshals were in the basement. Miles entered the marshals' office and dropped the warrant paperwork on their receiving desk. "Problem solved."

They headed for Miles's boarding house to get fishing gear. They were a little surprised to see Mabel strolling along,

"Tired of the Presidio?" Miles asked.

"Not at all. Are you gentlemen heading off to Berkeley?" Mabel asked as she twirled around a yellow parasol. She was wearing a peach colored dress Miles did not recall seeing before.

"Why would we be doing that?" Miles asked.

Her parasol stopped twirling. "The War Department

wanted someone over there arrested."

"They've got guys in suits. Why do they need us? We're tired. We're going fishing," Miles said.

"Oh no." Mabel looked worried. "I was supposed to encourage you to go and arrest that man, but I never thought you'd kiss it off this fast."

"Why not just come fishing with us? I heard the salmon were running last night. They don't come into the surf very often," Miles invited.

"While I'm sure that's fun for you, smelling like fish guts and getting sand in your shoes, I really was sent to make sure you guys handled that warrant," Mabel insisted.

"Warrant, schwarant. The marshals serve warrants all the time. What could possibly go wrong? He's an academic of some sort," Miles said. "They're usually harmless."

"He's the freshman dean," Mabel said. "We've just been through some horrible things with them."

"Freshman dean? In charge of those horrible freshmen?" Miles asked.

"That's what I said. The warrant was mainly an excuse to bring him in for questioning." Mabel lowered her parasol and folded it up. "Very well. I can't force you. Go catch your fish. Maybe Mrs. Wilson will even cook it for you. I certainly cannot arrest them as I am not a federal law enforcement officer. I guess I'll return to the Presidio. They have cottage cheese for lunch. No matter what I order, some private brings me cottage cheese. Do you know what I think of cottage cheese?"

"Uh, I have an idea," Miles relied.

"And I think some poor private is going to need a clean uniform shortly." She started for the cable car drop off.

"Maybe, what say we go fishing over in Berkeley and maybe just check up on the marshals while we're at it?" Major Yeats suggested.

"Thank you, major," Mabel said.

"I think we just saved some poor private's life," the major said.

"No, Major Yeats, if that private brings me any more cottage cheese he's going to find it in places on his body he doesn't even know he has."

"We'll just catch the ferry," Miles said.

"If we hurry," Mabel added. Apparently she had invited herself along.

Miles knew Mabel didn't need the ferry. He also knew some things were very difficult to explain about her.

The ferry chugged along. The bay was especially choppy for some reason. The black smoke belched out of the smokestack, but the steam it created barely seemed to move the ferry. "At this pace they'll run out of fish," the major said. No one laughed. Then, mercifully, the ferry pulled up to the pier and they were able to disembark.

Miles said, "The Science Building is right there on the corner. I seem to recall this guy's name on one of the doors."

"Upstairs or downstairs?" the major asked.

"I never went upstairs," Miles said.

"That helps."

They were almost at the door when two shots rang out. A university police officer came running out the door, then collapsed on the pavement. Mabel sort of took a quick glance at him, then shook her head. The three of them crowded next to the wall of the building.

Then another shot rang out. That was followed by two more, somewhat louder rounds. Then the door opened and two men in suits with badges looked around, then took refuge next to the building as well.

"Don't worry folks, we'll get this taken care of," one of the newcomers said. "Jacob Brewster, United States Marshal."

"We're with the United States Treasury," Miles said. "Well, she's not, but Major Yeats and I are."

"Never met one of you fellows before," Brewster said. "We were serving a warrant on some little bald guy and he started shooting. Never saw that coming."

"What's with the campus cop?" the major asked.

"We needed directions. He don't look so good."

"He ain't," the major said.

"Do you have a plan, Marshal Brewster, or are you going to just crouch against this wall all afternoon with your hand on my butt?" Mabel asked.

"Thankfully, it's spring break and there aren't many

students around."

"Yes, we know that," Mabel said.

"They usually run out of ammunition about now," Brewster said. "Then they're a lot easier to apprehend." At that point, the marshal noticed something. "She's armed. She's got a gun."

"We know that," Miles said. "What's your point?"

"Just didn't expect that. Next you'll be telling me she's with the Secret Service or something," Brewster said.

Miles shook his head. "Of course not. She's with the War Department, Intelligence Office."

"So, this is your warrant?" Brewster asked.

"I didn't realize he'd be violent," Mabel said. "Want me to take care of it? I'm sick of just standing here?"

Before anyone could answer, Mabel ran through the door. There was a shot fired from one gun, then two more rounds from another. Then the door opened and the subject of the arrest warrant came rolling out onto the pavement.

"Okay already. Damn it lady, I give up."

"Ezra B. Cunningham, you're under arrest," Brewster said.

"It hurts," the prisoner said.

"Where are you hurt?" Brewster asked.

"She shot me in the balls. What is it with you women?"

"The bullet ricocheted off a globe of Mars that's in the office. It didn't even break the skin," Mabel said.

"And that's another thing, she pulled my pants down," the prisoner complained. "What is it with you women?"

"I had to see if he was bleeding and he isn't," Mabel replied. "And I wasn't going to mention your shortcomings, but you brought this subject up."

"And you got arrested by a girl, Get up," Brewster said.

"I'm not going anywhere," their prisoner declared.

"College students!" Mabel yelled. "Those horrible students!"

"Who's afraid of some college twerps?" Brewster asked.

A blue beam of energy sliced right through a light pole, bringing it down on top of them. Ironically, it was the prisoner, Ezra B. Cunningham who the light pole landed on.

"You idiot," one of the students yelled. "You got the dean."

"What the hell was that?" Brewster asked.

"Some kind of Martian weapon," Mabel said.

The expression on Brewster's face hardened. "You didn't think to mention they have Martian weapons?"

"Well, we're sorry about that. That's why we came to help," Mabel said.

"I was wondering why you people were here," the marshal said. "These here students have a powerful weapon, but I figure they don't know nothin'."

"Agreed," Major Yeats said. "But how do we disarm them? And Miss Saunders, I thought you and Miles reported the freshmen were killed at that barbecue?"

Mabel nodded. "I believe these are what you call upperclassmen. No stupid hats."

Miles looked across the quad at the English Building. "Oh crap." Two more campus police officers were racing toward them, each carrying billy clubs. "They're sitting ducks."

The major tapped Miles on the shoulder. If the students were focused on the campus cops, they might be distracted just long enough. Both Secret Service agents began a direct charge toward the student holding the Martian weapon. Just as the student opened fire on the approaching campus police, the major fired at the student. The student fell to the ground. The rest of the students appeared to be unarmed and began to scatter.

Miles picked up the Martian weapon. "I guess we should turn this over to the War Department."

"I reckon so," the major agreed.

"It hurts," the disarmed student said.

"Well, when you try and kill people, that's what happens." The major glanced at the boy's wound. "You'll live. Unfortunately."

Miles took the Martian weapon over to Mabel. "Uh, just a moment." He dropped the weapon on the sidewalk and stomped on it with his boots. He continued this until it sounded like something broke inside. He then picked it up and handed it to Mabel. "Compliments of the United States Treasury."

"Thank you, I guess."

The marshals decided to take the injured student and the deceased Dr. Cunningham over to the campus infirmary. Mabel went back to the Presidio. Miles and Major Yeats went fishing on the Berkeley Pier. They caught two salmon, which they took to the boarding house and convinced Mrs. Wilson to cook them—but not clean them. Miles was tasked with that chore.

About two hours later, Miles woke up. He wasn't all that surprised that Mabel was in bed with him.

"Colonel Crabtree was really mad you broke his toy."

"And you missed the salmon."

Mabel let out a sigh. "Nobody said anything about salmon."

"I don't think the army needs weapons like those."

Mabel pointed out, "Maybe not, but he's not happy."

"You still working for them?"

"For now, although I may go back to hell." Mabel put her head on Miles's shoulder. "Life sure is complicated on Earth. In hell everything is pretty simple and nothing ever changes."

"Tomorrow is pork chop night."

"What's that got to do with me?" she asked.

"I think guests cost twenty-five cents," Miles said. "I can check with Mrs. Wilson."

"Well, you sure know how to show a girl a good time," Mabel said.

"No need to get sarcastic."

Mabel licked his ear. "I wasn't. I'd love to have pork chop night."

"Oh."

"I live in hell, remember?"

"Well, you're never there."

"Hell doesn't have pork chop night."

"Good point," Miles agreed.

26
HOME SWEET HOME

November, 1884
The Presidio, San Francisco, California

Mabel completed the form DS-9 report and placed it on Col. Crabtree's desk. She noticed a woman was sitting in the outer lobby. "May I help you?"

She stared at Mabel for a moment. "I was here to see Col. Crabtree about the file clerk position."

Mabel did not even know there was a file clerk position. "Did you have an appointment?"

"Not really. The lady in the office upstairs said to see him."

"I see. I don't know how long it's going to be. He's in a very important meeting," Mabel said.

"Well, I guess I'll try another time," she offered.

Mabel asked, "Can I get your name so I can let him know you were here?"

"Sure. It's Frances Waters. I'm staying at Mrs. Wilson's Boarding House over on Ocean Street."

That got Mabel's attention. She took a closer look at what could be competition. Had to be around thirty-years old. That made her kind of an old maid. But she was very pretty—raven haired and stunning green eyes that had the sparkle of emeralds. She spoke with a southern accent. Mabel would have guessed New Orleans. She could be trouble. Mabel liked being the prettiest woman in the room. She liked it a lot. This could definitely be trouble. "Well, I will let him know." The door opened. Col. Crabtree entered. "Uh, Colonel, this is Frances. She's here about the file clerk position." Just a minute later and Mabel could have pitched the information into the trash and been done with her.

Frances didn't like the long trek from the Presidio. Even on the cable cars it was quite a ways. But Mrs. Wilson seemed nice.

The place was very clean. And meals were included for what a lot of places wanted for just a room.

She'd found Mrs. Wilson sawing a limb off an apricot tree. A really fine looking horse was wandering around the yard.

"Hello, you had a room for rent sign out front."

"Oh, I'll be right with you."

Frances went over to the tree. "Can I help?"

"It's pinching the saw blade. Can you hold it up?"

Frances pushed. The saw finished its business and the limb came off.

"We had a lot of wind. It broke off some of the limbs. Now, would you like to see the room?"

"Yes," Frances said. "Does he always wander around free like that?"

"Oh, that's Paul. He belongs to one of my tenants. He doesn't really go anywhere. Back to the barn, Paul. Supper's not for another hour." Mrs. Wilson smiled. "Sometimes, he seems like he understands me."

"He's certainly a fine looking horse."

Paul let out a snort and shook his head.

Miles got home on time for once. He fed Paul, then headed to his room to relax until supper. It was chicken night. He could smell one roasting in the oven.

As he went down the hallway he noticed the door next to his was open. There hadn't been anyone living in there for a while. He noticed a nicely shaped rump was sticking in the air. The rest of the woman was bent over unpacking a trunk. He knocked on the door frame. She fell over on the floor.

"Uh, I didn't mean to startle you. I live next door."

She picked herself up off the floor. "I'm Frances."

"Miles O'Malley." He extended his hand and Frances shook it. "Nice to meet you."

"I just got in. This seems like a nice boarding house."

Miles nodded. "I've been here quite a while. Well, supper is in about two minutes."

"I'll be along," she said.

Miles went to the dining room and was greeted by a slice of roasted chicken, green beans and a baked potato.

Frances arrived a few minutes later. "Everything smalls so wonderful."

Mrs. Wilson asked, "Frances have you met Miles yet?"

"Yes, just a few minutes ago."

Mrs. Wilson introduced Mrs. Ripkin, she was the old lady who smelled funny, and Admiral Updike, a retired navy man who was nearly blind and muttered to himself. A harmless bunch.

"Mr. O'Malley, what is it you do for a living?" Frances asked.

"Call me Miles. I work downtown at the courthouse for the United States Treasury Department."

"I just moved here from New Orleans," Frances said. "I'll be working at the Presidio as a file clerk for the army."

"That should keep you busy," Miles said.

"How so?"

"I've been to the Presidio. They have a heck of a lot of files."

27
THE GRINDSTONE

Miles awoke as usual. He wondered what fate awaited him, what sort of assignment was lurking on Wentworth's infamous clipboard. As near as he could tell, the new Wentworth was pretty much the same as the old Wentworth. And he was, as usual, already there when Miles arrived at the courthouse. "Morning, Wentworth."

Major Yeats was there already. He'd been gone so much Miles had gotten used to being the only agent in the State of California. It was a good thing nothing ever happened in the southern half of the state. Los Angeles was a fairly small town that was not expected to amount to much. And they lacked water for growth down there.

Frances looked up from her desk. She'd been reading the army's directive on filing, form 941-A. She looked up from her reading and noticed Mabel was approaching and carrying a large stack of files. They were dropped on her desk, 121 in all. Frances wondered how she could carry so many files.

"These need to be filed downstairs in the blue filing cabinets," Mabel explained. "Not the brown ones, the blue ones."

"Okay." It took two trips to get them all downstairs. Frances wondered what the difference was between the blue filing cabinets and the tan filing cabinets. There was no sign or label to indicate the difference. Working for the army sure wasn't like the Brice & Stern Commodity Brokers. If only Raymond Brice wasn't such a perverted man. After the fifth time he tried to expose himself to her, Frances decided to leave and get as far away from New Orleans as she could.

As she was filing, she looked out the window and noticed Miles and a tall red-haired man walk by the window—each one was carrying a shotgun. A few seconds later, five soldiers came by the window—each of them were also carrying shotguns.

Then a smallish person with a hood over his head came by—followed by two more soldiers with shotguns. They all entered the building next door. That was what the army quaintly called the stockade. In reality, like almost all of the Presidio buildings, the stockade was a jail built with thick stucco walls when it had been a Spanish fortress.

Then Mabel came by the window and went inside the building next door. A minute after that, Col. Crabtree did the same.

One nice thing about working at the Presidio was she got ridiculously cheap meals at the mess hall. Things were going so well.

But, there was this Mabel person. Twenty years ago there was a Mabel person in Vicksburg. This one looked just like her. She hadn't aged a single day.

And then there was this Mabel person's sister, Kevin. Frances remembered watching her kill 160 men with her bare hands—well 159, the captain, she shot him in the rectum with his own revolver. She thought those memories were over, but seeing Mabel brought them all back from the Civil War. She wanted to run away and hide somewhere. Somehow, she struggled to make it until the end of the day.

The boarding house was such a refuge from the stirred up emotions she was feeling. Except for the fact Miles was sitting in the parlor at that precise moment reading the *Examiner*.

"Hi Miles," she said

"Well, hello, Frances. Tonight's pork chop night. It's my favorite."

"I can't wait. I was so happy to find a place with meals included," Frances said.

"Well, I've been here quite a while. I wouldn't want to live anyplace else," Miles said. He put down his newspaper. "It's about that time."

Mabel came out of the stockade at ten o'clock, five minutes after she entered it, if the Waterbury clock on the wall was accurate. She walked across the immaculate parade grounds and stopped to talk to Col. Crabtree. Then Mabel returned to the office.

Frances went back to her work. Miles had been right about the ridiculous amount of files the army possessed. But figuring out the system was getting easier and easier with each passing day.

"Miss Saunders?"

"Yes?" Mabel replied.

"Uh, what is your title here?"

"My title?"

"We all have titles. Everyone in the army has titles."

"Special Assistant to the Commanding Officer." Mabel took a sip of coffee. "Doesn't tell you much, does it?"

"Not really," Frances replied. "I've never worked for the government before."

"It's something," Mabel agreed. "Don't worry about it."

"Well, I've got to go downstairs," Frances said. Through the window she noticed two naval officers walking along with a couple of MP's. They all went inside the stockade. Ten minutes later, they came back out.

Frances couldn't really help but be curious what was going on in the stockade. It seemed odd that the navy was involved. You just didn't see the navy on an army base. It wasn't natural.

28
THE PRISONER

"**Do you have** a good enough view?" It was Mabel.

Frances nearly jumped out of her skin. She hadn't heard anyone.

"Perhaps I could get you a chair to gaze out the window," Mabel offered. "Curiosity is definitely not what the army pays you for."

"You haven't aged a day," Frances said.

"Excuse me?"

Frances repeated, "You haven't aged a day. I last saw you at Vicksburg. And you still look exactly the same. How is that possible?"

"I do not believe we have ever previously met. Perhaps you're confusing me with someone else?"

Frances went back upstairs and opened her handbag. She took a small framed picture and pushed it near Mabel's face. "You took this picture of me at Vicksburg, twenty-one years ago."

Mabel recognized the photograph immediately. "The bugler? You're that kid who was the bugler, for the south? The one pretending to be a boy?"

"That's me. The same kid in this picture you took twenty-one years ago. How is that even possible?"

"Uh, the only answer I can give you is no answer at all."

"You'll just have me fired and I'll just fade away?" Frances asked. "I get it."

"No. Nothing of the sort. Go ahead, tell them. They won't believe you. They won't even believe you were a bugler. You're dressed as a boy." Mabel headed for the stairs. "Get back to work. Even the Confederate Army would not hire a girl and attach her to a combat unit. The army just doesn't make mistakes like that."

The two sentries looked her over suspiciously. They seemed

surprised she was on the list. Mabel signed in and was admitted to the stockade. She walked past four more guards and then came to a large cell at the end of the hallway. "How is he today?"

"Who can tell?" the sergeant replied.

Mabel nodded in understanding. "He has such a sunny disposition. Well, open up."

"You heard the lady," the sergeant said.

Two guards removed metal poles that had been holding the metal door. The lock on the door was unlocked and the door opened.

"It seems a lot of trouble. I am not that strong to break out of this hell hole you have placed me in," the little green man with glowing eyes said in his language.

It was a language Mabel could easily understand and speak. "I'm sorry you are uncomfortable. The locks are not to keep you in here."

He stared at her for a moment. "Then what are they for?"

"To keep more of your people out."

"Oh. We are not used to keeping prisoners. It is barbaric."

"What do you do with them?" Mabel asked.

"We kill them," the Martian said. "Anything else is uncivilized. I wish I could die. Being held prisoner is worse than death. And having to speak to a woman—that is the biggest humiliation of all."

"Perhaps so, but I am the only person who speaks your language." Mabel started for the cell door. "May you die in your sleep."

"May your children be diseased," the Martian replied.

Mabel wondered about the translation on that last comment, then decided she did not really care. Who would know if she was off?

Finally, mercifully, it was time to go home. "Happy Thanksgiving," someone yelled. It was the fifth time she'd heard that. Mabel failed to understand the point of the holiday. Of course she had no family to gather with.

"Happy Thanksgiving!"

"Thank you Mrs. Wilson," Mabel said. "I'm here to see Miles."

"It's Nadine?"

"Mabel, actually."

"Oh, of course. He's still eating breakfast. He's in the dining room."

"Thank you." Mabel noted, as she entered the dining room, that Miles was able to fit an astonishing amount of pancakes into his mouth with one bite. She did not recall ever seeing him eat pancakes before. She would be happy if she never saw it again.

"What plans do you have for today?" Mrs. Wilson asked.

"We were going to the Presidio. The army band is having a concert," Mabel explained.

"Will you be back in time for Thanksgiving supper?" Mrs. Wilson asked.

"Of course," Miles said.

Miles and Mabel headed out the door. "There's something odd about her," Frances said.

"Now, if you don't have something nice to say about someone, don't say anything at all," Mrs. Wilson replied.

"And I sure don't recall any concert on the schedule for today."

"Well, the army does have a band. The late Mr. Wilson and I used to go there for Independence Day concerts." She picked up the plate Miles had been eating off. "That man sure loves pancakes."

"Maybe I'll check out this so-called concert," Frances said.

"Well, have fun, dear."

●

They climbed off the cable car. It was still a few blocks to the War Department Office of Intelligence. "Col. Crabtree thinks we should try some form of torture."

"In reading the reports, it would seem having to talk to you already is torture," Miles said. "Torture is seldom an effective means of gathering information. I have serious doubts about it."

"I hated telling Mrs. Wilson about a non-existent concert," Mabel said. "But I had to think up something believable right on the fly there."

"Your country thanks you," Miles said.

"I'm not even a United States citizen," Mabel pointed out. "It's not really my country."

"I do tend to forget that," Miles said.

Mabel got her key out and opened the office door. "It's so quiet here today."

"What do they eat?" Miles asked.

"Who eat?"

"Martians."

"Well, the one we're holding won't eat much of anything. He likes steamed carrots and pineapple. He's refused everything else we've offered him—including tea and coffee." Mabel picked up a piece of cake from a small table next to where they kept the coffee. "This didn't go over very well. He says it's disgusting."

"What are they going to do with him?" Miles asked.

"I don't know. Col. Crabtree doesn't seem to be getting much guidance from the War Department or the White House."

"Well, since it's Thanksgiving, should we requisition some turkey for him?" Miles asked.

"Let's make him happy. Hah! Steamed carrots and pineapple," Mabel decided. "Yummy time."

They went to the mess hall, which was nearly deserted. Most of the soldiers had been given leave for the entire Thanksgiving weekend. Mabel handed a special medical request form to the cook.

"What sick doctor makes his patients eat steamed carrots every day along with pineapple?" the cook said. "Boy, if I get assigned to this Doctor Saunders I'm running straight out the door and heading for Mexico. What's he got, anyway?"

"I don't know," Mabel said. "Probably some horrible disease of some kind."

Mabel carried the tray over to the entrance of the stockade. It seemed odd there were no sentries out in front. Then there weren't any inside, either. And there weren't any at the cell, either. And the cell door was wide open.

Miles drew his revolver from his inside holster. "Where could a little green man go? He kind of sticks out."

"He must've had help," Mabel said.

"Who would help him?" Miles asked. "He's not exactly

charming and it's not like he has a bunch of friends to hang out with in the city."

Mabel didn't waste any time in offering one suggestion. "Those horrible college students. They seem to worship these people—and I use that term people loosely."

They went back to the stockade entrance. "Oh pooh. What is she doing here?"

"Thought I'd check out that so-called concert. Only there isn't one."

29
TURKEY DAY

"**I would suggest** you go home," Mabel said. "There are things going on here that do not concern you."

"You two are up to something," she replied.

"And what we are up to does not concern you," Mabel warned. "Go home. You are a file clerk. This isn't your problem"

"Whomever you had locked up in that building has escaped," Frances said.

"And that is why we want you to leave. You are interfering with my investigation," Miles explained.

"Investigation? You said you work for the Treasury Department."

Miles showed her his badge. "I do. And for the last time, go home."

Frances started to walk back toward the cable car drop off. She was too bewildered to know what else to do. She had no idea there were Treasury lawmen, but Miles did have a badge. She'd thought he stamped forms or something.

After Frances left, Mabel opened the safe. She extracted a wooden box.

"They let you have the combination?" Miles asked.

"Nope. Don't need one. You forget who I am."

"Now that she's gone, I like your college boy theory. And they're off from school for Thanksgiving as well," Miles said.

"Assuming it's still confined to Berkeley students, how are they getting him out of the city? There's a limited ferry schedule to Oakland today and none to Berkeley. Even if they did use a ferry, he's kind of conspicuous. And I wonder where our sentries are."

Mabel let out a sigh. "Frances, you are one stubborn woman. I can hear you in the supply room and I can smell that perfume you wear. Get out here."

"What is going on? Who is it that escaped?" Frances asked.

Miles looked at Mabel for guidance, then decided to answer the question. The prisoner was captured when a Martian spacecraft crashed a few days ago. He was under heavy guard and, frankly, I don't know how he got out. Now, will you keep your mouth shut and go home?"

"Do they travel in glowing spheres?" Frances asked.

"Yes, they do," Miles replied.

"I saw one once at Vicksburg." Frances pointed at Mabel. "She was there. She saw it, too,"

"And that is irrelevant," Miles said.

"It got out of the thing. I saw the creature. I know what they look like," Frances said.

"We've got things to do," Miles said. "Actually, there is something you can help us with."

"Anything," Frances said.

Madam Veronica looked over Frances suspiciously. "One more time."

"I am looking for Col. Crabtree. There is an emergency at the Presidio."

"We get a lot of girlfriends and wives looking for their husbands. You're from the Presidio? The army's hiring girl soldiers now?"

"I'm not a soldier. I'm a civilian employee. I urgently need to see the colonel."

"I'll be right back," Madam Veronica said.

Two minutes later the colonel arrived at the door. "What is it Miss Waters."

"Secret Service Agent Miles O'Malley sent me. The Martian prisoner has escaped."

"Oh shit." He turned and yelled down the stairs. "Come on Wentworth. The Martian's got out!"

Mabel and Miles arrived at the ferry pier about two minutes too late. The ferry was already underway. It was packed with men wearing gold and blue shirts. And they were singing something.

They had someone in a bear suit. The school's mascot was the California Golden Bear, now extinct. "They could have our quarry in that suit. No one would notice him."

"Let's grab a fishing boat." Miles grabbed Mabel and sort of dragged her along to the commercial piers just west of the ferry pier. He was thrilled the *Murphy Giant* was docked and the skipper seemed to be on board. "Captain."

The skipper looked over at Miles. "I know, it's an emergency. Who is it this time, the Queen?"

They were just about to push off when a carriage rode up to the pier. Frances, Wentworth, and Col. Crabtree got out.

The Oakland Ferry was just putting along. The fishing boat was making good time on overtaking them when someone spotted them and yelled, "It's that army guy!" A blue light flashed out toward the fishing boat, but missed.

"Damn, how many of these things are there?" Mabel asked. She opened the box she'd taken from the safe and removed a hand-held Martian weapon. She sent a beam of energy back at the college students. They could hear somebody scream, but there were too many students to figure out who it was. The blast caused enough commotion that the ferry came in too fast and struck the Oakland pier, sending college students flying.

"Grab that bear mascot!" Col. Crabtree yelled.

In the commotion of the crash, people seemed confused and dazed. The guy in the bear costume turned out to be a guy in a bear costume. Then Mabel noticed there was a stack of ice chests stacked up on the ferry as well. She opened one.

"Ew!" Frances opened another one, then a third ice chest. They all contained freshly butchered meat. "Uh, Colonel."

"What is it Miss Waters?" He was trying to direct the arriving Oakland Police to contain the college students.

She pointed at the ice chests. "These are your sentries! What's left of them, anyway."

"No."

One of the students said, "Yeah, we were gonna cook them up tonight for Thanksgiving."

The colonel said, "And we thought the naval academy was bad. O'Malley, where's our escaped prisoner?"

"No idea, sir."

"Well search the ferry," the colonel ordered.

"We're on it," Miles replied. He and Mabel started for the stairway but never made it.

"Uh, Miles, come quick," Frances pleaded. She was on the far side of the ferry. Something glowing was approaching from out in the bay. It was completely underwater, but it was impossible to tell much else about it.

"If only the navy was here and they had some of their torpedoes," Col. Crabtree said. Then the glowing thing was gone. "I suspect we will not find our escaped Martian prisoner."

"These Martians are rather crafty," Mabel said.

An Oakland Police Sergeant asked Miles what they wanted to hold the college students on. He answered, "Conspiracy to commit murder, tampering with a cadaver. That should do for now."

"What about cannibalism?" Frances asked.

"Not technically a crime in California as I understand it," Miles said.

They were seven minutes late for Thanksgiving supper at Mrs. Wilson's. Frances and Miles had a strange lack of appetite.

"Did you enjoy the concert?" Mrs. Wilson asked.

"No," Frances replied. "It wasn't all that great."

"Oh, that's too bad."

After looking at the freshly carved sentries it was hard to get an appetite. Miles did manage to down two slices of pumpkin pie.

Mabel didn't eat much over at Madame Veronica's, either. She sort of moved her food around on the plate.

"Not hungry?" Madame Veronica asked.

"Not really."

"Have something to do with whatever dragged Col. Crabtree out of here?"

"Uh, yeah. A prisoner escaped from the Presidio stockade. And they cut the guards up. They were going to eat them."

Madam Veronica stopped eating. "That's appetizing. So much for dinner."

"Yeah, it is. I find myself thinking about my sister. She loved cooking and eating people," Mabel said.

"My word."

"She's no longer alive. But she really liked to carve up folks."

"Mabel, you come from a strange line of people."

"All families are strange," Mabel countered. "Sorry I ruined your dinner."

30
LEFTOVERS

Miles opened his eyes. He couldn't read his clock. It didn't glow like some of the clocks being sold at the Emporium. Miles suspected they were using a product called radium to make clock dials glow. He didn't know a lot about science, but felt uncomfortable with the concept of radium, which was highly radioactive.

Thanksgiving had been a bust. The cannibalism had left no one craving food that day. So Miles had no idea what time it was. He was also pretty sure Mabel was sitting in his chair. "That creeps me out."

"What does?"

"That you sneak into my room and sit there and watch me."

"I like watching you sleep."

"It still creeps me out."

Mabel came over and sat on his bed. She actually had clothes on. "At first, it was kind of fun having a job. Now, I'm thinking about going back to hell."

"What brought this on?" Miles asked.

"Today. Those horrible students. Those damned Martians."

"The United States needs you, Mabel. You can speak their language," Miles reminded her. "No one else can do that."

"When angels get too involved in what's going on here on earth, it always causes trouble."

"Yet you keep turning up. And now you want to run off back to hell?"

"This catching cannibals and chasing down Martians is not me really."

Miles sat up. "Welcome to my world."

There was a loud pounding on the wall from the room next door.

"What is her problem?" Mabel asked. "I should go over there and give her a piece of my mind."

Miles whispered, "She seems to think we're talking too loud."

"Have you slept with her yet?" Mabel asked.

"No."

There was another bang against the wall.

"Excuse us, we're trying to talk in here," Mabel said. Mabel kissed Miles. "She'll never satisfy you the way I can."

Miles smiled. "When you're feeling blue, what cheers you up is a nice game of poker."

Her eyes kind of lit up. "I haven't been by the Palace Saloon in a while."

As usual, Miles found Wentworth busily filling out some government form. "Morning Wentworth. You survived the holiday, I take it." Miles poured a cup of coffee. They kept a small potbellied stove going to both warm the office and make a pot of coffee now and then.

"Just barely. A bunch of college kids killed soldiers at the Presidio and intended to eat them. Half of them escaped when the ferry crashed into the pier. We'll be rounding them up for weeks. The Martians are preparing to invade Earth. I don't know where Major Yeats is. And the payroll money is late."

"So, it's just another day in the Secret Service," Miles said.

"Pretty much," Wentworth agreed.

About the Author

David B. Riley has written seven novels and over 100 short stories which have appeared in magazines and anthologies around the world. He writes horror and science fiction. David is also the editor of sixteen horror, science fiction and weird western anthologies and publishes the annual fiction magazine *Science Fiction Trails*. He currently lives in Tucson, Arizona.

Also from David B. Riley and Hadrosaur Productions:

Legends of the Dragon Cowboys

www.ingramcontent.com/pod-product-compliance
Lightning Source LLC
Chambersburg PA
CBHW021922170626
46807CB00007B/2942